BETWEEN FIRE AND FROST

CRIMSON ICE
BOOK 3

WILLOW FOX

SLOW BURN PUBLISHING

Published by Slow Burn Publishing

Cover Design by GetCovers

Edited by Marla VanHoy

Proofread by Ami K. and Jen S.

ONE

LUCA

She fucking left me.

I'm sick to my stomach with dread, anger, despair as I crumple the note and throw it in the garbage bin.

"I can't believe she broke up with me in a note."

Anger boils in my blood and I yank my bowtie off, undoing the buttons on my tuxedo.

There's not going to be a wedding today.

Dante will be thrilled. He didn't even want me to marry Harper.

He tried to get her to marry Ashton.

I'm, however, crushed. I'm not sure running away is the better of two options: marry Ashton or flee, because marrying me must have been horrifying.

I feel like I might actually vomit.

I turn toward the door, brushing past Ashton as I storm out of the room. The house feels incredibly small and I hurry outside, needing air to breathe.

Fresh air isn't enough, but the chill numbs me and dulls my senses. It doesn't lessen the ache in my heart.

Tears threaten my vision, but I don't want anyone to see them, not Ashton, not Kensley, and certainly not my father.

The door swings open behind me.

I don't dare look to see who is chasing after me.

I'm raw inside.

I'll never forgive Harper.

She can run, but she can't hide.

Like a blizzard, I tear back into the house, demanding my father. "Dante!" My voice bellows with a roar as I feel the anger flowing through me.

Heat radiates from my body. My bowtie is gone, the jacket unbuttoned, and I'm still sweating.

Dante hears my voice, or maybe it's the hurricane that follows me as his men swarm like I need help.

I don't have to say it.

Dante stares at me, and it's like he knows.

Does he know because he figured it out on his own or had he been told?

"I want Kensley detained," I growl and point at the girl in the dark-purple dress standing just a few feet away.

"What?" Her eyes widen, and she takes several steps backward but knocks into Moreno.

He grabs her by the arm, dragging her down the hallway.

"Please, no!" she screams, fighting for her life.

I'm fighting for mine.

For my wife.

Correction.

For the wife I should have had and the boy who was to become my son.

Ashton steps closer. "Are we sure we should be doing this now?" he asks into my ear.

"This is on you." I glare at him. "If you hadn't demanded she marry *you*, maybe she wouldn't have run away."

Ashton shuts up.

Dante's gaze flits from Ashton to me. Clearly, he's surprised I'm privy to what goes on under his roof.

Turns out, we all have secrets.

Kensley is dragged down to the basement holding cell, kicking and screaming.

No one stops them or helps her.

I glance around and see no sign of Harper's parents. The only guests here today are all aware of whose house they're in—the mafia's.

They're family friends, not acquaintances. The wedding guests are either those who work for Dante or have come at his insistence.

They all know he's mafia.

None dare to intervene.

They're not foolish enough to think they have a shot in hell at calming down a mafia boss. But Dante is relatively calm, and I'm the one fueled with anger and betrayal.

Hatred burns brighter and hotter than love.

Betrayal burns my skin, licks my tongue, and fills me with hate.

I storm down the basement stairs, finding Kensley secured to a metal chair, her legs and arms already bound. Moreno was quick with the ropes and chains. It's not his first interrogation, although Matteo is our typical interrogator.

But I want to be the one questioning Kensley.

I deserve to be the one doing the interrogating.

"Please," she pleads with Moreno, and I gesture for him to step away.

"Give us a minute," I say and nod for him to take the stairs and go back up.

There are tears in Kensley's eyes, and she struggles to catch her breath. Her cheeks are flushed, her body trembling.

Moreno heads up the stairs, leaving me alone with Harper's best friend.

"Please, you have to help me," she pleads.

I kneel beside her, reaching her eye level. "Why would I do that?" I seethe, my fists clenched tight at my sides. "You knew Harper's plan."

She's silent.

Seems I'm right.

"How long has she been planning to leave me?" The words cut like a knife into my heart as I say them out loud.

"I don't—she didn't want to, but your father."

I shake my head, not believing Kensley. "My father didn't send her away. She chose to run. To embarrass me on my wedding day."

Kensley's brow pinches. "She loves you. It's why she left. You read the letter."

"I read that she wanted to end things, that she doesn't want me to chase after her. Where did she go?" I growl and lean closer, tipping the chair backward. My hands grip the metal, keeping Kensley from falling.

Her eyes widen as she gasps for air. "I don't know! I let her use my credit card," she admits far too easily. "You really are mafia."

My gaze tightens. "Did Harper tell you that?" I tilt my head, replanting the feet of the chair back onto the cement floor.

"She told me everything," Kensley whispers, staring up at me. "But she left out the part where you're the monster."

Her words cut deeper than the betrayal of Harper's leaving.

I never wanted to become my father, but torturing Kensley, the anger burns through me hotter than fiery coals in a roaring flame. "She shouldn't have run."

"You don't love her," Kensley says, refusing to back down.

I see the fear behind her pale-blue gaze. I've frightened her, but she doesn't cower.

She straightens herself in her seat, defiant. "She left because she loves you."

"That's the stupidest thing I've ever heard," I growl at Kensley. I tip her chair back, and her eyes widen.

She knows if I let go, she'll smack into the cold concrete, likely hit her head. She's leaning forward, trying to brace herself for the moment of impact.

But I don't remove my hands from the metal chair.

"She didn't want to force you into a life with her and Zeke."

"But I want that life!" I shout at Kensley, as if he she can somehow tell Harper while being restrained on the metal folding chair.

I slam the chair back down on all fours, and she bounces but doesn't fall over.

Kensley is breathing hard, her body trembling from the adrenaline.

"I shouldn't have trusted Harper to keep our secret."

"I swear she only told me because she knew she could trust me," Kensley says, defending her.

"She should have trusted *me!*" I shout.

"Your allegiance is to your father, your family. She told me everything about how you're being forced to work for your father. Harper was trying to give you another life. A better life."

I step back, needing to get away from Kensley. "It's all lies." I can't listen to her. She's trying to get into my head, confuse me, make me see things that aren't as they are.

"I swear to you, she loves you. That's why she did this—she's throwing her college education away, her stability. She has nothing while on the run."

I head for the stairs, taking them two at a time, leaving Kensley restrained.

"I have to find her."

I need to find her before Dante or his men track her down.

They're not going to be as forgiving.

"Did you get anything out of the girl?" Moreno asks as I step out of the basement.

I hesitate, deciding whether I want to do this alone, but think better of it.

Anything Kensley told me, she'll easily reveal to Moreno or any of the soldiers who question her.

"She gave Harper her credit card. Run the information, we'll be able to locate her." I don't divulge that Kensley knows about the family business. At this point, bringing her down into the basement, tying her up, she'd have figured it out on her own.

I glare at Nova as she comes racing around the corner. Apparently, she's gotten wind of what's happening.

"Are you okay?" she asks, looking exasperated.

"No," I growl, my gaze tightening on her.

Nova and Harper had become friends over the past couple of months.

"Did you know?" I snarl, stepping into her personal space.

She shoves me backward. “No. Harper kept me in the dark about her plan.”

Moreno watches the exchange between us for a moment before he and Dante hurry down the hallway to his office. I’m sure they’re planning on tracking Kensley’s credit card. Harper would need it if she were planning on staying at a hotel.

“Really? Because you two have been pretty cozy lately. Best friends, if I recall.” I want to believe Nova, but right now I don’t trust anyone.

Nova rolls her eyes.

She’s not the least bit afraid of me. She folds her arms across her chest. She’s dressed in the same matching gown as Kensley, deep purple with black trim. They were both to be bridesmaids for our wedding.

It burns my insides, realizing that there won’t be a wedding.

I didn’t even want to get married, but the rejection, the humiliation, it aches in every ounce inside of me.

I had an out.

Harper could have married Ashton.

It's what my father wanted, demanded of Ashton, but instead, she chose herself over me.

There's no relief, just melancholy.

"Get over yourself, Luca." Nova doesn't back down. "The wedding was a foolish idea from the start. You only agreed to it to keep her alive. Don't forget that!"

What started out solely as an act of protection became so much more.

Harper means so much more to me than just keeping her alive.

I wanted to marry her.

To spend the rest of my life with her.

Yes, there were times I was distant.

It's hard to be thrust suddenly into parenthood.

She has a son, and that mere thought, let alone the act of taking care of another person, a child, terrifies me. I never want to become my old man.

I'd tried to keep some distance from Zeke and from Harper.

But every time we fell back into patterns, climbing into bed, kissing, touching, I fell deeper, harder, faster, for Harper.

And now she's torn out my heart and left me with a fucking breakup letter.

"Go get stuffed," I growl at Nova and storm off to find Dante.

Hopefully by now, he's come up with Harper's location.

I waltz into his office without so much as a knock, as if I own the place.

One day I will, but not today.

Dante raises an eyebrow, surprised, but he doesn't scold me.

Another first for today.

Moreno stands silent in the corner of the room, the darkness lurking over him.

"Looks like they're in a small town southwest of here. There's a receipt for some diapers and snacks from a rest stop."

"I'll go check it out," I say and head out of my father's office.

"Luca," Moreno calls after me.

I glance over my shoulder.

"You might want to change first."

Ashton comes with me while Nova stays back with Kensley.

I've yet to untie Kensley from the basement. I don't know whether Moreno or another one of the soldiers will question her.

It's no longer my problem.

If she hadn't helped Harper run away from our wedding, then she wouldn't be subjected to our family's wrath.

Serves her right.

My heart is frosty and chilled from the betrayal.

I hear the crinkle of paper, and I glance at Ashton as

I'm driving in the direction of the rest stop where Harper was last seen.

It's unlikely she's still there, but Dante assured me that he'd call as soon as she makes another purchase.

It's only a matter of time, and at least we'll be close.

"What the hell is that?" I growl, but I already know the answer. He fished the breakup letter out of the garbage.

"Just something you might want to talk to Harper about."

I snort and grip the steering wheel tighter as I shift uncomfortably in the driver's seat. My foot is hard on the gas, trying to make up for lost time.

Harper has a couple hours' headstart.

It has to be why Kensley showed up. It wasn't just to give us Harper's letter, but also to buy time for her friend to get away.

"Why didn't Harper just go to her parents'?" I ask, glancing at Ashton.

"That'd be the first place we'd look for her. She *is* putting their lives in danger by bailing on the wedding," he reminds me.

I don't think she liked her parents very much, or maybe it's just that they weren't getting along recently.

Harper rarely talked about her mom and dad. I certainly didn't push the conversation. It's not like I'm close to my family, albeit for different reasons.

My phone rings, and I answer it via Bluetooth through the car speakers.

Dante gets right to the point. "We've got a location on her phone, but it looks like she left it on the bus. It keeps pinging from here to campus and back."

Explains why she didn't answer my texts.

Did she leave it on purpose to throw us off, or had she accidentally dropped it between the seats?

"Any new purchases?" I ask.

"Nothing yet. Kensley mentioned a bus ticket that she gave her cash for, but Harper insisted on not telling her where she was going," Moreno says.

They seem to be on speakerphone, sharing information.

"Did Kensley say anything else?" Ashton asks.

I glare at him.

"No, Nova brought her back upstairs against my authority," Moreno rumbles, and I can imagine he's pissed as shit at his daughter.

She's brave—I'll give her credit for that—and a bit insubordinate.

Ashton shifts in his seat, looking a bit restless. We've been driving for a couple of hours already, but I don't intend to stop until we get to our destination.

"It's fine." Dante clears his throat, and I sense there's some brooding tension.

Dante hated when he couldn't control me. I can't imagine he's keen on the fact Nova is going around and disobeying orders, doing whatever the hell she likes.

She's going to land herself in a shit ton of trouble if she's not careful.

"Kensley couldn't tell us anything we don't already know," Dante adds. "We sent her home, put surveillance on her phone. We'll know if she reaches out to Harper or vice versa."

I glare at Ashton.

Had my father done the same to me or Harper?

Another hour in the car and we pull up to the rest stop. I step out, stretch my legs and head straight in for the cashier, hoping he can give us some information.

"Good afternoon," the clerk says, chewing a wad of bubble gum. He barely looks old enough to run the register.

He pops a bubble and glances me over. "Can I help you?"

"We're looking for—" I begin, and Ashton steps up to the counter, interrupting me.

"My sister ran off with her son. He's about two," Ashton says and gestures to about Zeke's height. "We're looking for her before her deadbeat boyfriend shows up and threatens her again."

The clerk's eyes widen. "Oh, dear. Yeah, I remember her. Cute girl. The kid was a terror, trying to grab everything off the shelves and screaming when she wouldn't let him walk on his own. She was on the bus that stopped in here."

"Do you know where that bus goes?" I ask.

He glances me over. "Are you really her brothers? You two don't look alike."

"Different mother," I say, forcing a smile. "We're just trying to protect her and the little boy."

"Bus goes to Las Vegas," the clerk says.

We head back out to the car, fill up the gas tank and then hit the road.

"Are you going to call Dante?" Ashton asks, watching me intently as we head back onto the main road. I put Las Vegas into the map app on my phone GPS, so we don't get lost. Hopefully, it's the same route that the bus takes.

"Wasn't planning on it," I say.

If I call Dante, he probably has acquaintances in Vegas. They'll be waiting for Harper long before we get there.

I'm angry with her, but I don't want anything happening to her or Zeke.

"Good," Ashton says and leans back, making himself comfortable.

I glare at him as I'm driving.

"What?" he asks, glancing at me. "You keep staring at me like I'm to blame for all this happening."

"You're not innocent."

"Whatever. Her running away isn't my fault." Ashton folds his arms across his chest.

"You kept throwing yourself at her, I'm sure that didn't help the situation."

Ashton unfolds the crinkled letter, reading it silently.

"It doesn't say anything about me in here."

I reach for the letter, but he plays keep away with it. If I weren't driving, I'd have it out of his hands in seconds.

"Fuck off, Ashton," I growl and elbow him in the side as I attempt to keep my hands on the steering wheel, mostly.

"For a guy *not* in love, you're a bit tense. And I know you were getting laid. So, it can't be that. Everyone in the house could hear the two of you clawing at each other like wild animals."

"You're an asshole, and I never said I didn't love her. Harper is the one making that assumption." Clearly, she doesn't know how I really feel, because reading that letter tore me up inside.

Ashton chuckles.

"You better be prepared to tell her those three words or this trip is a huge waste of time."

TWO

HARPER

At every turn, I feel like I'm being watched.

Am I paranoid? Probably, but it's hard not to be when I'm running away from my wedding and I'm supposed to marry Luca, who is mafia born and bred.

Which is my fault. At least in part.

Luca had disowned his father until I screwed things up and forced him to propose, to keep me and Zeke safe.

I kiss Zeke's forehead. He's seated in his car seat, and he's been restless for the past two hours.

He's also burning up.

I thought it was from the heat pumping into the bus and his winter coat making him overheated. Now, I'm thinking it might actually be a fever.

His cheeks are rosy, and he's been crying and fussy for most of the trip. I remove him from his car seat and cuddle him, trying to settle him down.

He's warm, sweaty, and still fidgety.

I kiss his forehead, and I'm certain he's running a temperature.

Another ten hours on the bus to Vegas is out of the question.

The driver announces that the next stop is a small town and we'll be there for half an hour if anyone wants to grab food before we get back on the road.

It gives me a chance to see if there's a hotel, someplace where we can lie low for a bit.

I bundle Zeke back up into his winter coat and boots. He's screaming at the top of his lungs, not the least bit thrilled, and neither am I.

A couple of patrons on the bus are glaring at me, and I give them an apologetic smile. We won't survive a drive to Vegas.

At the next stop, I disembark with the backpack over my shoulders, Zeke holding my hand and the car seat in my other hand, filled with our recent purchases from the rest stop, consisting of snacks for Zeke, some baby Tylenol, diapers, and wipes.

It's blustery outside, the air whipping at me, and Zeke is inconsolable as the cold chill beats at us.

I lift Zeke onto my hip, holding him against me. He buries his face in my jacket as I survey the small town.

There's a motel not too far in the distance, across the street from the fast-food chain. I head for the motel, opting for a room. At least if I can get Zeke settled and rested, perhaps tomorrow, we can take the next bus.

Although I don't have my phone to purchase a bus ticket and there appears to be no bus station nearby.

That's tomorrow's problem.

Right now, I'm more concerned about Zeke and his apparent fever.

I manage to secure a room, using Kensley's credit card, and retrieve the key.

Zeke is fussing the entire time. "It's okay. We're going to rest soon," I say.

He's already missed his afternoon nap. He's a joy to be around when he follows his routine but add a fever to the mix and all hell breaks loose.

Not that I should be surprised.

Today hasn't been a typical Saturday for any of us.

After we get settled and I drop off our things, I take him across the street to grab a quick bite to eat. I'm starving, but I've been giving Zeke snacks to try to settle him down. I doubt he has an appetite anyhow.

I order a burger and fries and get Zeke a kid's meal, in hopes that he'll get some protein in him. Crackers, pretzels, and chips aren't exactly sustenance.

Zeke sits in my lap while I shred his chicken fingers, making them bite-sized pieces for him to feed himself.

He's sniffly and tear-stained, but he grabs the chicken with his fist, palming it before shoving it into his mouth.

I'm relieved that he's quiet for a few minutes, which gives me a few seconds to take a bite of my burger. I'm absolutely famished. I didn't eat anything for breakfast, and it's already nearing dinner time.

It's dark outside, but not quite Zeke's bedtime. It's still a little early. He finishes the last bite of his chicken and reaches for my fries.

"You've got fruit," I say, pointing at the cut up fresh fruit bites on the napkin for him to eat.

He wrestles forward, squirming for my French fry.

"Okay." I relent and rip a tiny bite off, so he doesn't shove the entire fry into his mouth. He grabs it, and his eyes widen as he tastes the salty delight.

He points to my fries, wanting more.

So much for trying to get him to eat healthy. I kiss his forehead. He's still warm, but it's not as raging as it was earlier.

Crying will also make him run a bit warm, and he's

settled down now that he's eating dinner. While it's not the best meal, it's better than snack food.

Sitting by the window, I glance out at the bus, the other patrons climbing back on, getting ready to leave town.

My breath catches in my throat when Luca's vehicle slowly pulls up in front of the bus, blocking it.

I glance away, hoping that maybe if I don't look in his direction, he won't see me inside the window of the restaurant.

But like a train wreck, I can't look away. My gaze is still on *him*.

My breath catches when someone is pointing at the hotel and then at the fast-food chain.

His gaze locks on mine, and he looks mighty pissed.

Luca tosses his keys at Ashton and stalks toward us.

Fuck.

Fuck.

Fuck.

Luca is fuming.

Ashton is moving the car, parking in front of the hotel.

Like a hurricane, Luca comes barreling inside, the anger rolling off him like steam on a chilly winter's day.

The look alone sends shivers down my spine.

It's frosty.

Bitter.

And reserved solely for me.

It's nothing to feel grateful about.

"You weren't supposed to come find me," I whisper, staring up at him.

Zeke throws his arms up at Luca.

"Dada," he says, and my heart hurts a million times more, hearing my son call him that.

Luca exhales loudly and tries his damndest to ignore Zeke.

I want to see his resolve crumble and for him to realize I'm not the villain.

"I can't believe you broke up with me in a letter. One that you didn't even have the courage to give me!" Luca isn't the least bit quiet, and the two other guests in the restaurant turn in our direction.

Sighing, I gesture toward the empty seat in the booth across from me.

"I'd prefer to stand," Luca bites out.

"I was trying to give you your freedom, Luca," I say, keeping my tone soft, disarming. There's no reason for me to fight with him.

Zeke squirms, growing restless in my arms, especially now that he sees Luca, and apparently, the kid has had enough of me today.

"My freedom?" Luca laughs darkly, clearly angry and hurting.

I should have realized what the consequences would be. I didn't intend to hurt him.

"I honestly thought you'd be relieved," I say, staring up at him.

"You don't know me at all." Luca shakes his head, fuming. "I've been prepared to throw my future away for you—"

"I didn't ask you to do that!" My voice raises an octave.

The door to the restaurant swings open, and Ashton slowly comes waltzing in.

"Dada!" Zeke says to Ashton.

Apparently, that's his new favorite word.

"Can I take him?" Ashton asks me as Zeke's arms are out, waiting to be held by anyone but me.

My little traitor.

Reluctance ebbs from me.

Ashton is as much mafia as Dante. He wouldn't have pushed the idea of marrying me if he didn't follow orders.

But I don't believe he'd hurt my son.

I've seen the way Ashton is with Zeke at home, chasing him around, playing peek-a-boo and tickle monster.

Zeke continues squirming until I relent.

"Yes," I say and hand him over.

Ashton carries him to the play area of the restaurant, trying to keep him away from the fighting adults.

"You risked everything, even Kensley's life. You were stupid telling her about the family," Luca hisses and falls into the seat across from me.

Shit.

I never expected Kensley to tell anyone.

"Is Kensley okay?"

I could never forgive myself if Dante or his men did anything to her.

"When I left, she was locked up in Dante's basement." He tilts his head slightly, eyes tight, studying me.

This isn't what I wanted.

If anyone should be chained up downstairs, it's me.

This is my doing.

Running away from the wedding.

Leaving Luca.

Divulging mafia secrets.

I'm the one to blame, not Kensley.

"It's not fair," I whisper.

"Life isn't fair. Quite a hard way to learn that lesson," Luca scolds.

"I had to trust someone."

He's glaring at me and then steals one of my fries. "You were supposed to trust me!" He pops the food into his mouth and chews rather aggressively.

"You never would have let me go."

"Now, you're catching on!" Luca snaps and shakes his head. He runs his fingers over the table, and I reach for his hand, hoping to draw some sense back into him and calm him down.

He blanches the moment I touch him and pulls away from me.

"Why are you here?" I ask, staring at him.

"Do you think Dante is just going to let you run away? He's hunting you down. You embarrassed the family. That doesn't just get swept under the rug."

I hadn't considered what my betrayal to the family might mean. I knew Zeke was in my custody and I'd keep him safe. My parents, they could fend for themselves. By not being close with them lately, it would protect them.

"I'll apologize, but I won't go back."

"You will," he says firmly. "Whether I have to carry you to the car or you walk, we're going back home."

"I don't—" My breath catches and I glance toward the playroom for Zeke.

He's oblivious to what's happening, thankfully. Ashton is keeping him busy.

"Run away with me," I whisper. "We'll take Zeke, maybe we can even get Ashton to cover for us."

I won't leave without my son.

"Ashton would never do that," Luca says, and he grinds his teeth, his jaw tight as he stares at me.

There's a coldness he exudes, and it sends a shiver down my spine.

"Dante won't let us leave. I've told you that, repeatedly. He has men all over the country who will do his bidding."

"What if we change our names—"

"You'll never be safe. We'll never be safe," he reiterates. "The only safe choice is to marry me."

I sit back in the booth and exhale heavily.

"Wow, that bad of an option," Luca says and laughs darkly. "You weren't saying that when we were fucking the other night."

I grimace.

He's angry with me.

I shouldn't have expected anything less. I'm not sure why I thought leaving him a note, telling him not to chase after me, would work.

"You don't want to marry me." I meet his frosty stare.

He silently swallows and his tongue darts out for a second, swiping across his top lip.

His silence is all I need to hear.

"Let me and Zeke go," I say. "Dante won't keep chasing me when he realizes I'm worthless to him."

Luca slams his fist on the table, growling at me. "You don't fucking listen!"

A staff member glances at us, and I can feel her worried gaze on me.

I force a smile, but she reaches for her cell phone.

She's watching, waiting to see if she should call the cops or if everything is okay between us.

"We need to get out of here," I whisper, keeping my voice down.

We're drawing too much attention to ourselves.

I glance out the window, and the bus is pulling away. My only choice is a ride with Luca and Ashton or stay in this small town until I can figure something else out.

"Good, finally some sensible words," Luca grunts and climbs out of the booth. He cleans up the tray of half-eaten food, and I grab Zeke's coat, heading toward the indoor playground.

Through the glass windows, I can see Zeke tumbling through the indoor jungle gym.

I reach for Luca's hand, hoping I can convince him to take us someplace safe, far from Dante.

He yanks his hand away, as if I'm fire and have the ability to physically burn him.

Luca grabs Zeke's coat in my hands and shoves the glass door open. "Come on, buddy. Let's get you ready. It's time we get back on the road."

We stop at the hotel first, grab Zeke's car seat and my backpack. I change Zeke's diaper and use the bathroom before we pile into Luca's car.

I sit in the back next to Zeke, who is protesting being locked into his car seat.

Dread fills my stomach as Luca turns us around and takes us back in the direction we came.

Breckenridge, Montana.

It seems there's nothing I can say that will convince him to drive us to Vegas or someplace else on the map.

I sit in silence, trying to reassure Zeke and settle him down as he wails for the next solid hour.

"What's wrong with him?" Ashton asks, glancing over his shoulder. He shifts in the front seat, trying to see why Zeke is hysterical.

I offer Zeke a toy, a snack, there's nothing that settles down his screams.

He's reacting the way I feel.

I run my fingers over his dainty hair. "I know, Zeke, I don't want to go back, either," I whisper. "It'll be okay. You and me, we'll get through this."

I glance toward the front of the car, and Luca is white-knuckling the steering wheel. He shifts, tense, as he glances at me in the rearview mirror.

But he doesn't say anything.

What is there to say?

He's made it clear that he's angry with me for leaving with Zeke. No amount of apologizing is going to fix what's been done.

Besides, I'm not sorry.

I was trying to help Luca out.

I'm just sorry that my plan went to hell.

Two hours into the drive, Zeke finally falls asleep. He's still running a low-grade fever, but the medicine seems to be helping.

Luca keeps the music on low, careful not to wake Zeke as we continue driving for a couple more hours before he pulls over to get gas.

He shuts off the engine, and Zeke stirs but doesn't fully wake up.

Ashton steps out of the car and heads into the gas station, while Luca pumps gas.

When Luca finishes, he opens the front door and reaches for his phone. From the backseat, I can tell he's texting someone, but I can't make out what's being said.

I think better than to ask. I'm not sure that I'll like whatever answer he'll give me.

We're another hour or so from Breckenridge, two hours from campus. I don't dare ask if Luca is driving us back home or to his parents' house.

I'm too afraid to speak, that I might wake Zeke and break the spell of his slumber.

As we exit the main throughfare, I realize we're returning to Luca's parents' home.

Shit.

Nausea sweeps over me, and as we pull to an abrupt stop in front of the Riccis' home, Zeke stirs.

Luca kills the engine, and I work on unbuckling a grumpy Zeke, who is fighting sleep.

When Luca steps out of the car, a cold blast of air assaults us, which further intensifies Zeke's cries.

"I know." I work on getting his coat back on from the backseat and zip him up to keep him warm.

Luca yanks open the back door on Zeke's side, and my little monster betrays me, clawing for Luca.

"Dada," Zeke wails as Luca lifts my son into his arms and Zeke buries his snotty face in Luca's jacket.

He carries Zeke to the front door. I try the car handle, but my side is child-locked.

Ashton opens the car door for me, letting me out.

They clearly didn't want me to try to escape. I button my coat and grab my backpack, hurrying after Luca and Zeke.

Luca heads inside, and I follow right behind him, helping remove Zeke's coat while he squirms in Luca's arms.

"Dada. Dada," Zeke keeps repeating while I wiggle his shoes off before removing my own.

Dante's footsteps click over the marble flooring. "Look who decided to return," he says, glaring at me.

"Luca, Harper, come with me, *now*," Dante seethes and turns sharply, heading down toward the library.

Luca doesn't release his hold on Zeke, who is fidgety and whiny, trying to get down, wanting to tear through the house.

But at least there are no tears.

At least not from him.

I'm fighting back the dread as I follow behind Luca, who is a solid several steps ahead of me.

He's practically left me behind.

We're no longer a united front. There's no pretending that we're in love or in a relationship.

Luca Ricci hates me.

Luca's mother, Nikki, is seated in one of the armchairs. When she sees us, she stands and hurries over to Luca, taking Zeke in her arms.

It's the first time she's ever offered to hold my son, and I can't help but feel my stomach tumble as I step closer, wanting to take him back into my arms.

I don't trust Nikki or Dante.

I don't trust any of them with my little boy.

Nikki seems to have the magic touch, though, bouncing him on her hip, smiling and making faces at him, which settles Zeke down.

She leans forward and kisses his cheeks and forehead, frowning. "He's burning up."

"He's been running a fever on and off all day," I confess.

"I'm calling the doctor," Nikki says, carrying Zeke with her out of the library.

"I gave him baby Tylenol," I say, trying to ease her mind.

I may be a shitty girlfriend, but I'm not a bad mother.

I want to chase after Nikki. I don't like that she's taken Zeke out of the room, but Luca grabs my arm, his grip solid and warm as he keeps me from rushing after Nikki.

“Zeke will be fine.” Luca’s words are meant to assure me.

I exhale heavily and try to take a moment to breathe as I glance through the open door where Nikki just disappeared, and Ashton steps foot inside the library, joining us.

Dante steps toward me, his cold gaze sending chills straight through my heart.

“You disappointed me, Harper. I don’t like being disappointed.”

It’s a warning.

I nod faintly, staring up at him, realizing that there is no running from this man, not today.

I tried, and I failed, miserably.

“I’m sorry; it won’t happen again.”

“I’d like to think not,” Dante says with a huff. “You’ll be getting married this evening.”

I turn toward Luca, eyes wide, waiting to see if he’ll

object and tell his father that he doesn't wish to marry me.

He's made it perfectly clear that he hates me.

"The wedding is still on?" I ask, my voice cracking.

"You didn't think you could run from our family, dear, did you?" Dante asks with the hint of a devious smile on his face. "You're lucky Luca and Ashton found you and it wasn't one of my men."

"I'm sorry." I'm quick to apologize. Maybe I can find another way out of this disaster.

Dante's gaze tightens.

"Apologies don't lessen embarrassment. You attempted to humiliate my family."

Luca's hand drops from my arm.

The coldness in the air sends goosebumps across my skin.

"That was never my intention," I say.

Do I try to explain that I was trying to help Luca? I doubt Dante cares about my intentions, and Luca certainly wasn't happy with me when he read my letter.

"I'm sorry," I say, hoping that maybe another apology will help ease the damage I've caused.

"I don't care about your apologies. They're meaningless," Dante scolds. "You will marry him, now."

"Now?" Luca's voice betrays him as he glares at me. He blanches.

"We informed all our guests that Harper was ill with a bout of food poisoning. You will wed Ashton tonight," Dante says.

Ashton?

"No!" I shake my head and glance back at Ashton, imploring him to stop this madness.

He doesn't wish to marry me.

And I don't want to be tied to him.

He cares for Nova.

I care about Luca.

It's a match made in hell, Ashton and me marrying. It can't happen. I won't let it. I'd sooner die than marry Ashton Rinaldi.

Luca hates me, but if I marry Ashton, everyone will hate me.

Nova will never forgive me.

Luca will despise me for marrying his best friend.

And Ashton will regret it for the rest of his life.

"You can't do this, sir," I say, pleading with him. "The agreement was that I was to marry Luca."

Dante's eyes flicker for a moment. "That was the agreement, but you've betrayed the family. Don't you think a punishment is in order?"

"You're going to punish Ashton for me running away?" I ask, shocked.

I knew Dante wanted me to marry Ashton. He'd gone to Ashton, ordered him, like I was just another assignment, but we'd agreed that it was foolish and stupid.

Ashton strides closer, his skin glistening and pale. He looks taken aback by the recent news of our impending nuptials.

Turns out, Ashton hadn't lied to me when he agreed to let the choice be mine.

But Dante has other ideas, and being the mafia boss, what he says, goes.

I reach for Ashton, taking his hands, staring up into his gaze.

"I'm calling in that favor you owe me."

THREE

ASHTON

How the fuck am I going to get out of marrying Harper?

I've never disobeyed a direct order, not from my father and certainly not from Dante. He freaking scares me.

Intimidating is an understatement.

"Sir, you can't think that me marrying Harper would be a good idea. Luca and Harper will be pining for each other, and it'll put me in a precarious situation."

Luca huffs under his breath, and I glare at him.

"They're sleeping together," I elaborate, as if that will change things. "For all we know, she could already be pregnant with his child."

Dante glares at Harper and glances her over.

"Are you carrying his child?"

She looks aghast at the suggestion. "I don't think so—"

"But she can't know for certain," I say, glaring at Harper. I'm trying to give her an out. Doing everything in my power to keep the two of us from being forced to tie the knot.

"I could be pregnant," Harper says and rests a hand on her stomach. "I mean," she glances at Luca, "the last time we—"

"We were careful," Luca growls and steps closer to Harper. "She's not marrying Ashton. He's not so much as touching *my wife*."

Harper's breath hitches, and I hide the smile growing on my face as I take a step back, trying to let the two of them sort through this little issue and keep me out of it.

"Your wife," Dante repeats, rubbing at his jaw. "You still want to marry Harper? After everything she's done to hurt you?"

"I fully intend on taking her as my wife," Luca growls and grabs Harper's hand a bit aggressively. He tugs her closer, and I've seen the two of them act in love before, but this is something else.

Possessive.

Heated.

Luca is fueled with a quiet rage destined to be destructive.

Dante is quiet, seizing the moment, deciding on what course of action he wishes to take. "Luca, you will wed Harper at once. Ashton, you will be a witness, and I will handle being the officiant."

FOUR

LUCA

Once Nikki returns with Zeke, standing against the wall, she keeps him quiet and calm.

There is a set of wedding rings on the bookshelf that we are provided, and I slide a gold band on Harper's ring finger as I say the required vows.

I can barely look at her.

Her eyes are on me, but I look everywhere but her face.

The pain rips at me, scolds me. This is wrong, but letting her marry Ashton, I could never allow it.

Once the ring is secured, I move my hand away, refusing to touch her for a second longer than necessary.

She shifts the weight on her feet.

Harper clearly isn't happy.

None of this makes me happy, either.

I'm still dressed in jeans and a sweater.

Harper's not even in her wedding gown. The moment feels like we're being robbed, but at the same time, I shouldn't care.

I don't care.

Dante recants the vows that Harper must say as she takes my hand and slides the ring over my finger.

Her hand is warm, while my fingers are ice cold.

I want to pull away, but she takes her time sliding the ring onto my finger, over past my knuckle, and she holds my hand as she says the required words.

The weight of the band is heavy, and I stare down at the mistake that will forever stare back at me.

This isn't a celebration of love.

It is a ceremony meant only to join us in marriage, a legally binding contract.

Nothing more.

And within minutes, we are wed.

"You may now kiss the bride," Dante says.

Glaring, I glance up at my father. "Is that a requirement to be wed?"

I have no desire to kiss Harper, let alone touch her.

From now on, she can sleep in Zeke's room.

Dante glances at my mother. "I do not believe so," he says.

"Very well." I drop Harper's hands, the rings burning onto our skin as I storm out of the library, needing air and plenty of space.

I head out into the backyard, the cold breeze a welcome after the unrelenting heat inside.

"How are you holding up?" Ashton asks as he steps outside after me. He hands me my jacket.

I take my coat from him, sliding it on over my shoulders, and walk to the edge of the porch, overlooking the backyard. It's quiet outside but cold. I can see my breath.

Staring down at the gold band, I twirl it with my thumb. The movement is subtle, the band a perfect fit.

It's just an object.

It doesn't have to mean anything.

"That good, huh?" Ashton quips and comes to stand beside me.

"Yeah, well, no thanks to you," I mutter. I turn my attention from the ring to Ashton. "Were you really going to marry *her*?"

"I was hoping I wouldn't have to," Ashton admits and rubs the back of his neck. "I don't have feelings for her if that's what you're worried about."

"You used to," I seethe, remembering when we were both crushing on the same girl.

It wasn't so long ago, which has me skeptical that his feelings are truly gone.

But Harper is mine now.

Ashton is smart enough to abide by the mafia code. You don't fuck with a brother's wife.

Jealousy creeps in, and I'm not even sure I understand why I care, because Harper did everything in her power to destroy me.

"Used to is a long time ago. I have my sights set on a different girl at Evergreen," Ashton says.

That garners my attention.

"Anyone I know?"

Ashton forces a tight smile. "She's way out of your league." He pats me on the back. "And you're married, so she's off-limits."

I roll my eyes.

"Is this because I gave you shit all last semester about keeping away from my little sister?"

Ashton's face goes slack, and he clears his throat. "I'm just saying, don't worry about my love life when yours is on fire."

"Seems like it's a bit more frosty than fiery. I'm never taking her to bed again," I grumble.

My best friend chuckles and eyes me with disbelief. “Hate her all you want; the best sex comes after that. I’ve heard the two of you going at it.”

“I’m not fucking her,” I growl.

Ashton throws his arms up into the air. “Fine. But if you won’t give it to her, some other guy eventually will.”

I glare at Ashton and shove him forcefully. “My wife won’t cheat on me.”

“Not at first,” Ashton says, “but come on. If you’re expected to be married forever, are you telling me you’re never going to dip your stick in someone else’s honey pot?”

I can’t listen to Ashton.

I storm back into the house and come face-to-face with Harper.

She’s cradling Zeke against her chest, rubbing his back in soothing motions as he fidgets against her.

I recognize the older gentleman speaking with Mom, and then he steps over, examining Zeke in the hallway.

He's a pediatrician, was my doctor and Nova's when we were growing up. I'm a bit surprised the guy is still practicing medicine, but he could have been brought out of retirement at Dante's insistence.

I step toward the wall, leaning against it for support as I watch the exchange.

Is something wrong with Zeke?

He uses his stethoscope to listen to Zeke's heart and lungs. Then he checks his ears, nose, and throat with his special light.

"I'll take a culture," I overhear as he grabs his bag and retrieves a long cotton swab. He gets Zeke to open his mouth, grabs a sample, and then hands the kid a lollipop.

Zeke was incredibly fussy on the drive back here until he fell asleep. I just figured he hated being buckled into the car seat and was protesting.

The doctor says something, jots down some notes, and glances at the test strip with the culture. I can't quite hear him. A few minutes pass, and then he scribbles down a prescription.

The pediatrician wanders back over to Nikki, exchanging a few pleasantries before she escorts him out.

"Everything okay with Zeke?" I ask, watching as he sucks on the lollipop, his eyes still red from crying and his cheeks tear-stained.

"Looks like he has strep," Harper says. "The doctor just gave us a prescription for some antibiotics."

I grab the prescription from her. "I'll run out and get his medication," I offer, heading for the front door.

"Luca, you don't have to—"

I'm gone before she can finish her sentence.

I need to get out, put some space between us. But when I get to the pharmacy, I realize I don't know any of the information to fill the prescription.

What insurance does Harper have for Zeke?

What's his date of birth?

Any allergies?

I'd call her, but my father still has her phone. He had one of his men grab it from the bus that she'd left it on.

I end up ringing Ashton, knowing that he's still at the house. He's not leaving without me, since I'm his ride back to campus.

"Where'd you run off to?" Ashton asks.

"Can you put Harper on the phone?"

"Your death wish," Ashton jokes, and I hear the phone switch hands.

Zeke is making sounds beside the phone, making it harder to hear Harper. "I need some information for the prescription," I say.

I have her walk me through the details as I fill out the form at the pharmacy counter. It takes longer than it should, and while I know Dante has a supply of drugs and medications in case of emergency, I'm not sure Zeke's sore throat classifies.

Not to mention the prescription is an oral solution, not a pill.

Unlikely he has the right dosage and medication for Zeke.

She takes a photo of the prescription card and sends it to me. The lady at the counter is less than thrilled, but when I explain we're newlyweds and our son is sick, she seems to be a little less heartless.

Twenty minutes later, I'm leaving with the prescription, and I grab a box of fruit-flavored popsicles for Zeke. They might melt on the way home, but at least they'll numb his throat and maybe quiet him down so we can drive back to campus tonight.

When I get back to the house, I hand over the bag of medication to Harper along with the popsicles.

"For Zeke," I say.

She opens the medication bag and administers the orange liquid to Zeke. He willingly takes it without too much of a fuss.

"Do you want a popsicle, buddy?" I ask, showing him the box with lots of colors and flavors. I let him point to the color on the box that he wants, which happens to be the hardest one to find, blue.

I tear off the plastic wrap, and he reaches for it, but so does Harper, holding onto the stick.

I have a feeling she's going to end up wearing most of it.

"Are you ready to head back home?" I ask.

"Yeah, I'd like to put him down to bed," Harper says.

"Let me find Ashton. Meet me at the front door in five."

I wander through the house, finding Ashton in the library seated with Dante.

"We're heading home," I say, interrupting their discussion.

Dante sighs. "How's Zeke?"

"He'll be fine." At least I hope he will. "We should get him to bed, though."

"This weekend, bring Harper with you. We're going to need wedding pictures. I also need you to sign this document," Dante says and gestures toward the table.

It's the marriage certificate.

Harper has already signed it.

Ashton has signed it as a witness, as has my mother. Dante signed it as the officiant.

Turns out, I'm the last to sign it.

My father shoves a black pen at me.

"Same as I told your wife, you're not leaving until the document is signed."

I scribble my signature and drop the pen on the marriage certificate.

"Happy?" I glower at him.

"Not particularly," Dante says. He reaches into his pocket and retrieves a cell phone. "Your wife's phone that she left on the bus."

I bite down on my tongue and take it from his possession, sliding it into my pocket.

"You can rest assured; there's nothing incriminating on her phone."

So much for privacy. "I wasn't concerned," I bite and storm out of the library.

Ashton is a few seconds behind me.

"We're heading home," I say and head for the foyer. I lace up my sneakers and slip on my coat.

Harper is helping Zeke get bundled before going outside.

I grab his little shoes and manage to finagle them onto his feet. It's not an easy task with a squirmy toddler who is dripping blue popsicle all over the foyer.

Dante will be thrilled, but he has staff who will clean it up for him.

I can't ever remember Dante cleaning anything himself.

Mom comes over to say her goodbyes to us, carrying the box of popsicles I left on the counter. "Don't want to forget these for Zeke," she says, like I won't be back on Friday night.

I've seen her more in the past couple of months than I did all of my freshman year.

"Thanks, Mom. Did Nova head back to campus yet?" I ask. I hadn't seen her around this evening, but maybe she's holed up in her bedroom studying.

"Moreno drove both Kensley and Nova home this afternoon."

"See you on Friday," I say, giving Mom a quick hug goodbye. While I'm not looking forward to returning, I'm true to my word.

I have to help Dante with the business. I'm not sure which I'm dreading more, taking on more mafia responsibilities or taking wedding photos with Harper this upcoming weekend.

Zeke falls asleep in the car, and I'm grateful for the quiet moments as we drive back to campus.

Harper is seated in back with Zeke; Ashton is up front with me.

I have the radio on low, careful not to stir Zeke. Ashton glances at me but doesn't say anything. He's probably watching his words, considering Harper is in the backseat.

It was dicey today.

Tomorrow probably won't be much better.

He turns the radio slightly louder to drown out his question when he whispers to me. "Do you think she's going to try to run away again?"

I glance in the rearview. She's staring at her sleeping little boy and doesn't seem to be paying us any attention.

Honestly, I hope she won't leave me.

It'll kill me.

But I can't know without a doubt that she won't get scared and flee. She's already left once.

"Can we not talk about it?" I glance at Ashton and then shift in my seat, sighing.

"Long day," Harper says.

I'm not sure if it's my body language, the heavy sigh, or Ashton's question that has her commenting.

Did she hear him?

When we get back to the house, Nova comes darting out of her bedroom, as does Liam.

"Did you find Harper?" Nova quips and then her eyes widen when she sees Harper holding a sleeping Zeke in her arms.

"Sorry," Nova mouths quietly.

Liam's smirking, his arms folded across his chest as he lingers in the doorjamb, clearly amused by all of it.

Great.

Glad I'm fodder for him.

Another spectator in our forced marriage who is going to want details.

Liam doesn't quite know all the details of what led up to the engagement, just that the marriage ended up being a necessity at my father's insistence.

That's all Liam needed to know to understand why I was getting hitched.

His father is also mafia; everyone who lives under our roof is either a child of the mafia or married into the family.

It's why we're all living together, and I suspect how we all ended up enrolled at Evergreen on full scholarships. There are no coincidences.

FIVE

HARPER

After twenty-four hours, Zeke's fever breaks, which is a relief because I can't send him to daycare if he's contagious.

I've been sleeping in Zeke's room, on the twin-sized mattress tucked against the wall.

Zeke seems to be thrilled with the company, climbing into bed with me every morning and even in the middle of the night when he wakes up.

Which means less sleep for me.

The kid sleeps sideways, hogging not only all the blankets, but also the entire bed.

Repeatedly, I've tucked him back into bed, but he keeps making it a habit to climb into my bed, which worries me because I don't want it to be a bad habit when he's a little older.

Luca barely speaks to me, except for the occasional nod or good morning when we see each other off—he heads to practice early with Ashton and Liam, I'm studying before Zeke wakes, and I have to take him to daycare.

I have a full day of classes lined up today—communication, astronomy, and statistics. As an advertising major, they're all required classes, but the comms class is by far the easiest for me.

I meet up with Kensley for lunch. It's the first time that we've seen each other since I left town.

"I heard you were back," Kensley says as I carry my lunch tray to the table.

She's got some bruising around her wrists, and when she notices me staring, she covers the darkened marks with her sleeves.

"It's nothing."

"It's not nothing." My voice drops lower. "Did they hurt you?" I ask.

Nova and Ashton enter the dining hall and head in line to grab pizza. We don't have much time to talk privately.

Kensley shakes her head. "Not physically. I mean the restraints left some marks, but it's nothing I can't handle. We shouldn't talk about this here."

"I still have your credit card." I reach into my backpack and retrieve it, passing it across the table to her. "I'll pay you back for everything—"

"I know. Don't worry about it right now." Kensley grabs my hand that's on the table, the one where I'm wearing a wedding band. "You went through with it," she gasps, the evidence staring back at her.

"Didn't have much of a choice." I refrain from mentioning how Luca's father insisted that I marry Ashton instead of Luca. That part hardly seems important now that I'm married to Luca.

"Shit," she mutters between bites.

I ordered a salad for lunch, not incredibly hungry, and picked at the lettuce. I've mostly eaten around it;

the diced carrots and cucumbers have gained more of my attention.

“How are you doing?” she asks, watching me.

“Fine. Luca’s not talking to me; well, mostly he’s ignoring me.”

“Sounds like a healthy marriage.”

I snort at her joke and reach for my water, taking a swig. “We’re sleeping in separate bedrooms. But I get it. He’s pissed.”

“He’ll come around,” Kensley says. “I mean, you’re married. He can’t go his entire life avoiding you.”

“I’m not so sure about that,” I grumble under my breath and stab at my salad.

“Hey!” Nova says as she grabs a seat at our table. “I heard the big news. Let me see the rock.” She holds out her hand, waiting for me to deposit my hand in hers.

I lift my left hand, which houses a simple gold band. “No rock. Just wedding bands,” I say.

“I can’t believe I missed the wedding! I’m going to kill Dad for making us leave the house early.”

Kensley shifts uncomfortably and pushes the remainder of her sandwich aside, uneaten. She seems to have lost her appetite, not that I blame her. I don't know exactly what she went through, but it couldn't have been good.

Does Nova have any inkling of what happened with Kensley?

"I'm going to head out. I have class and I should get there early; it's across campus," Kensley says, excusing herself as she grabs her backpack and then her trash to discard.

"I'll catch you later?" I ask.

But she doesn't meet my stare.

"Yeah, maybe. I know where you live. If I have time, I'll stop by." Kensley jets out of the dining hall like it's been set ablaze.

"That was odd," Ashton mutters and glances at Nova. "How's the pizza?

"Pretty decent for cardboard." Nova glances over her shoulder in the direction Kensley disappeared. "Is everything okay with her?"

I shake my head. "I don't know. She had some marks on her wrists—" I say.

Ashton clears his throat. "Moreno escorted her down into the basement when we realized she'd helped you run away."

I push the salad aside.

The small appetite that I had vanishes.

"Moreno tortured her." I glance up at Nova.

"Dad wouldn't do that. He insisted that we return to campus to protect Kensley. It's why he drove us home himself. He was keeping Matteo from interrogating her."

"Did you see the marks on her wrist?" I reiterate.

"No," Nova says. "Dad wouldn't hurt one of your friends. I mean, I'm sure he sat her down for questioning, demanding to know everything she knew, but he wouldn't *hurt* her."

"I'm not so sure," I say, reaching for my water and taking another sip.

"I know my father," Nova says. "He follows orders,

but he wouldn't hurt Kensley. He wouldn't hurt a girl. That doesn't follow his code."

I bite my tongue. Sure, they wouldn't hurt a girl, but they sure as hell would kidnap a little boy.

Nova is either naïve or in denial. Either way, discussing it any further seems irrelevant.

"If you're upset about what happened in the basement, maybe you should ask Luca," Ashton says. He finishes the slice of pizza and wipes his hands on a napkin, his dark gaze staring right through me.

"What do you mean?" I ask.

"Luca was the one doing the questioning. He interrogated Kensley."

The air leaves my lungs, and I can't breathe. "Where can I find Luca?"

"We both have philosophy after lunch. You can walk with me. I normally run into him on the way to class."

After lunch and before my next class, I ambush Luca on his way to philosophy. Turns out, both his class and my statistics class are in the same direction.

Ashton gets the hint and falls behind a few paces, letting me catch up with Luca and allowing us some semblance of privacy.

"You look frosty," Luca says, glancing at me.

"I'm steaming," I snarl and fall in step with him. "You interrogated Kensley?"

Luca clears his throat. "That's a bit harsh a word. I questioned her."

"She has marks on her arms. She was restrained," I say and grab Luca's arms, stopping him from walking any farther. I need answers.

"I didn't put her in that chair, Moreno did. I just asked the questions."

"You also didn't let her go," I say, guessing he wasn't there to save her.

Luca shrugs.

I hate that I'm right, that he found it necessary to interrogate her because of me.

"Did you hurt her?" My hand remains firmly planted on his arm.

He yanks away from my touch. "No!" Luca huffs and takes a step back.

I wait to see if he's going to run away from me, but he doesn't. He stands there, avoiding my harsh stare. His gaze is on the ground and then his feet. "She knew things. You told her about *my family*."

I inhale sharply. "I didn't have a choice."

His gaze lifts to meet mine. It's filled with fury. "There's always a choice."

"Right. Like I could have asked you for a bus pass and money to get my ass out of town." I roll my eyes at him, annoyed that he thinks spilling that secret came easy to me. I was terrified for Kensley, but I did what I thought was best for all of us.

He still doesn't see that.

Instead, he's fueled with rage and hatred toward me.

"I told you, anywhere you run, my family will find you."

Turns out, he was right about that. Luca and Ashton managed to track me down. "I should have paid in cash," I mutter.

Luca growls and invades my personal space, his hand on my hip. "You should have told me your plan. I could have helped you escape."

"But you just said—"

"I know, but I would have led them astray."

I pull away from him. "I don't believe you," I say. "You kept telling me there wasn't another choice. Anywhere I run, they'll find me. Your family has friends in other cities, states, probably other countries."

"All truths," Luca says matter-of-factly.

I toss my hands up into the air. "You're full of shit, Luca. You'd never let me go!"

"You're right. As my wife, you are bound and tied to me, forever."

There's a fire in his blackened gaze, and I step back.

Luca Ricci hates me.

Most of my classes this semester aren't too bad,

except for statistics. I'm drowning in numbers and formulas.

After a terse discussion with Luca and then a dreaded statistics class, I'm seated in the study lounge in the house, going over the day's homework assignment.

It's all a bunch of nonsense.

Kind of sums up my life.

"You look either confused or really constipated," Ashton says as he walks by.

"I hate statistics."

"Oh, I took that last semester. Super easy."

I snort. "For you, maybe. Any chance you took notes in that class?" Maybe I can make sense of his notes from last year and use them to understand what I'm trying to accomplish, because right now I'm drowning, all over again.

I thought economics was hard, but that was a breeze compared to this class.

"None that I saved. Here, let me help." He pulls up a

chair beside me and glances over the information that I have written down.

"Yeah, this is wrong." He points at the homework assignment and my first two answers.

"Okay." I exhale heavily and stare at him, frustrated. "I spent an hour on that. How can it be wrong?"

"I mean, it's wrong," Ashton says. He flips through my textbook and tries to explain to me how the example isn't matching what I'm doing. "You're just like way off," he says and gestures with his hands.

"And you know this because—"

"Because I got an A in statistics and my minor is in forensic accounting. I know numbers. I can do them in here," he says, pointing at his head.

"Show off."

Ashton helps me erase my answer, and then he walks me through doing it the correct way. Which I'm not quite sure I understand.

He explains it again.

Overwhelmed, I scoot my chair back.

It's not he's a bad teacher; I'm just not getting it.

I glance at the clock. We've been at it for over an hour, and I need to pick up Zeke soon from daycare and then work on dinner.

"You're done," Ashton says. "I've seen that look in Nova's eyes when the information doesn't seep in and your eyes glaze over."

"You help Nova study?"

"We both have psychology together. It's more of a mini study group, just the two of us," he says with a wicked grin.

I roll my eyes and hold up a hand. I don't want to know if his idea of studying doesn't involve books and school assignments.

"Glad things are working out for you two. When are you going to tell Luca?" I hate hiding it from him.

It's only been a few days, but he's still angry with me for running off, leaving him on our wedding day.

Apparently, my intentions don't matter, only what I did, which was humiliate the family.

He's been terse around me, disappearing the moment I try to speak with him about anything. He's not home for any meals, making it an easy excuse not to sit down and talk.

And while I know he's busy with hockey, so are Ashton and Liam, and I see them more than I see my own husband.

That word feels weird as it skates through my mind.

Husband.

Until death do us part.

The only vows that he probably feels true to, because I know that loving me isn't one of them.

"Take a break," Ashton says, pulling me out of my thoughts.

"Yeah, I need to pick up Zeke."

"If you ever need help with him," Ashton offers.

"Thanks. You're a good friend, even if you're lying to your best friend." I glare at him, wanting him to tell Luca about his relationship with Nova.

It's selfish of me, I know, but if Luca is focused on Nova, maybe he won't be so mad at me?

The front door swings open, and I close my textbook. I really should put everything away. I'm done for today, my homework abandoned. I didn't get it done—maybe after dinner when I have more time to stare at it blankly because I suck at statistics.

Luca walks past us with his backpack and does a double take when he sees Ashton and me in the study lounge.

His eyes tighten as he glances at the two of us, like we've been caught doing something immoral. "What the hell is going on in here?"

Ashton stretches his arms and rests one hand on my shoulder, holding me like one might hold a girlfriend.

I glance back at Ashton, wondering what the hell he's doing.

"Ashton saw I was struggling and offered to help," I say.

Luca huffs and shakes his head. "She doesn't need your help, Ashton. You've done enough as it is, stay away from my wife!"

Ashton stands and stalks around the table, coming to face Luca.

He isn't afraid of him, nor does he back down.

"Why? Are you jealous?" Ashton tilts his head, sizing him up. "The way I see it, your wife needed a little one-on-one *tutoring* and I was willing to *give it to her*, unlike you."

Innuendo drips from his words, a sinful smile spreads across his lips.

Ashton is taunting Luca and loving every minute of it.

My mouth drops, wondering why the hell Ashton is being a jerk. He knows our relationship is tremulous at the moment. Is he trying to make matters worse?

Luca drops his backpack and lunges at Ashton, wrestling him to the ground as he starts throwing punches at his best friend.

Ashton blocks the majority of them with his arm, but one gets slammed into his ribcage and he grimaces.

"Stop it!" I scream, jumping up from the table. I don't

know how to break two boys apart when they're fighting, least of all without getting hit.

Ashton shoves Luca away, and they both get back up onto their feet.

"Why the hell are you fighting?" I glare at Luca, demanding to know what's gotten into him.

"Why is *he* tutoring you? If you need help, you come to me!" Luca's clenching his teeth and I refrain from rolling my eyes.

"Are you—jealous?" I can't fathom what Luca has to be jealous about; he doesn't even want to be near me. "He's just trying to rile you up. Nothing deplorable is happening between us. He's just helping me with my homework. Ashton took statistics last year."

"So did I." Luca's top lip twitches with a snarl. "If you need help, I'm your husband; I'll help you."

Oh, he's definitely jealous. His muscles flex in his arm, and his jaw tightens.

It's actually kind of hot, not that I'd confess that to him right now.

He's steaming and has wanted nothing to do with me since the day of the wedding.

Is this Ashton's way of trying to help, stirring up trouble to get Luca to notice me again?

"Okay," I say and shove everything into my backpack. "Can you help me tonight with my statistics homework, Luca?"

"Fine," he grumbles. "After Zeke is in bed."

It takes a while to get Zeke down. He keeps climbing into my bed in his room and wanting cuddles. I lie down with him in the adult bed, getting him to settle in and shut his eyes. I rub his back, finally relieved when his breathing evens and he falls asleep.

I carefully carry him into his toddler bed, tucking him in before slipping out of his room, our room.

My clothes are still in the dresser where Luca sleeps, but my bed has been in Zeke's room for the past several nights.

I'm not sure when Luca will want to share a bed with me, sex aside, just being in the same room with him tenses him up.

And he thinks he's going to help me with my statistics homework?

I head into the study lounge and spread my books and assignment on the table in front of me.

It all feels familiar, only because I was already in here earlier today, not because I know an ounce of what I'm doing in statistics.

Turns out, I also don't know what I'm doing with my marriage, either.

Luca plays hockey on Thursday night; perhaps if I show up with Kensley or Nova at the game, I might be able to get things between us back on track.

Not that I'm expecting him to want a replay of me fucking him while wearing a Narwhals' jersey, but just treating me like a friend instead of ignoring me or yelling at me would be a nice change of pace.

Luca wordlessly steps into the study lounge.

His hair is wet, his sweatpants sit low at his waist as he puts a t-shirt on, and I can't help but stare.

"You're drooling," he says to me.

Is he trying to lure a response from me? Because it's working. I don't want to feel the attraction, but it's impossible to ignore as I stare at his muscles, his toned body, the line that goes down to where his sweatpants rest.

"Asshole," I mutter.

He comes around to sit next to me at the table, and I try not to drink in his scent, sandalwood and amber. It's definitely the shampoo he's using, but fuck, that aroma stirs all of my senses in ways that it shouldn't.

Not when he hates me.

I shift on the chair, hoping he's oblivious to the early signs of my arousal. Just having him next to me, the heat radiating off his body, I feel like an animal in heat, ready to pounce.

Down, girl.

He doesn't want me.

"Statistics," I say, but my voice croaks, and he turns his head to stare at me.

I take a breath, try to regain my composure and force a smile. "Thanks for helping me with my assignment."

"That's a little premature," Luca says. "I haven't helped you yet."

He silently reaches for the homework assignment and reads it over to see what we're working on.

And just like last year, he's right there, explaining everything to me, walking me through what the professor is looking for and how to come to the right conclusion.

He's brilliant, smart, and sexy as hell.

I want to hate him, but I can't.

We spend an hour together, actually studying, which consists of Luca tutoring me in statistics and helping me catch up on today's class where I felt like I didn't learn a damn thing.

He stretches and reaches for my notebook. My stomach grumbles as he turns through the pages and shakes his head. "You wrote all this down in class, but it's wrong."

"It's what the teacher said," I counter.

"Yeah, well, it's wrong."

"Okay, Einstein, do you want to correct it?" I hand him my pencil.

"Not particularly." Luca stands and heads out of the study lounge.

I expel a sigh and rest my head on the table.

I guess he's done with me.

A minute later, the sound of crinkling draws my attention, and I lift my head, glancing up.

Luca returns with a bag of potato chips, shoving the salty snack at me. "Your stomach is making sounds, and I can't concentrate when you make noises."

"Thanks," I say, reluctantly taking the bag from his grasp. I pop a few chips into my mouth and crunch away.

The sound of my annoying crunching doesn't seem to bother him. He's diligently fixing my notebook, cleaning up my scribbles and comments so that they're accurate. He's flipping through my textbook along with my notebook, making sense of the chaos in front of him.

Is Luca actually being nice to me?

I opt not to ask, keeping the question to myself.

I offer him a potato chip, and he opens his mouth, letting me pop one inside while his hands continue erasing and then rewriting, before turning the page in my textbook and then in my notebook, doing it all over again.

"I think that once you have notes that are accurate, you might actually better understand what you're learning," Luca says.

"I'm not a bad note taker," I counter.

"No, but I think you didn't quite grasp the concept and then you've built on the framework, which has just made everything a mess."

"Story of my life," I say.

Luca turns his head, tilting it as he glances at me. "Don't do that."

"Do what?" I ask, not sure what I've done to offend him.

"Turn this into everything being your fault. Because it's not." He turns to face my notebook, flips the textbook page, and then erases my notes before reworking what I messed up.

"Pretty sure I'm the reason we're in this mess," I say. "I went into the basement when I shouldn't have—"

Luca sighs heavily. "Yeah, well, I shouldn't have even let you come to the compound that night. We're both to blame."

I want to reach out, run my hand across his back. I can see the weight of it, the struggle that he's endured. It isn't just me dealing with what's happened. We're in this situation together.

While it's hard not to feel guilty that I'm the cause, I can see he has remorse, and I don't want him regretting any of it.

"It's not your fault," I say and reach my hand out, placing it on his arm.

"No, it's both our faults." He stares at me and then down at my hand on his arm. His gaze is enough to burn me, and I flick my hand away, putting it back in my lap.

"Bet you don't feel that way about me running away on our wedding day," I mutter.

Luca's jaw is terse. His shoulders tense, and he stares down at the pages of notes, his voice rough and raw.

"Believe it or not, I had a feeling that you wouldn't show up."

"I'm sorry," I whisper, and I want to touch him, but I don't want him hating me either.

I'm trying to give him space, let him simmer down and come to realize that we're married. Unless he plans on taking another girl to his bed—and I don't think he'd do that; eventually, he has to want me again.

This self-loathing and hatred of me can't last forever.

"Don't apologize," he growls. "Not when you don't mean it."

I press my lips together and think better of telling him that I do mean it. That if he had read the letter, then he should know I did it for him. I was trying to set him free, let him live without being under his father's shadow.

Silence fills the void between us, and when I glance at him, it's hard not to stare. His neck muscles ripple from the tension he's holding in his shoulders.

I should let the quiet continue to fill the air, but I can't seem to remain still.

"I saw Kensley at lunch today."

Luca swallows, and his hand pauses as he's fixing my notes.

"She has bruises on her wrist," I whisper, and he flinches. "Do you know anything about that?"

"Don't ask me questions that you don't want the answers to," Luca snaps. He puts the pencil down, flips through a few more pages in the notebook. He's caught up and slides the notebook in front of me to review the new items.

"You interrogated her."

"I did what was necessary to find you."

"I told you not to chase after me," I say, and he turns his seat to face me.

"No, Harper, you wrote me a letter. You didn't tell me anything."

"Semantics."

Luca is shaking his head. "Do you honestly believe that if I just let you go to Las Vegas or wherever you were running away to, that my father wouldn't have dragged you back?"

That's what I'd been hoping. It's why I used Kensley's credit card and not the one that my parents had given me for emergencies.

It didn't occur to me that they could track down her purchases and figure out where I went.

"I'm sorry. I shouldn't have run."

"Again, don't apologize when you don't mean it," Luca says, glaring at me. I'm surprised he hasn't gotten up and stormed off.

He's still so incredibly angry, but I'm not sure there isn't also hurt and grief locked up inside his heart.

"About Kensley, what happened. Did you—hurt her?"

I noticed the marks on her arms. Does she have any more under her clothes? I didn't notice whether she wore makeup to cover any bruises, but I hadn't been looking that closely, either.

"You think I'm my father," Luca says and pushes the chair back.

I've lost him.

He stands and takes a step back. He doesn't leave the study lounge.

It's just the two of us in here, but there's no door, no actual privacy. Anyone can hear us fighting, and I've been trying to keep my tone down so as not to wake Zeke.

"I didn't say that, Luca."

"You didn't have to!" He runs a hand through his dark hair, and his breathing grows louder. I can hear him across the room, each gasp that he takes. His hands clench into fists at his side.

"Kensley had bruises. I just, I want to hear it from you. Tell me what happened."

"I didn't fucking lay a finger on her!" Luca shouts at me.

I momentarily close my eyes to try to steady my racing heart. They're only shut a fraction of a second before I blink and I'm staring right back at him.

"She had bruises on her wrists," I say, not the least bit afraid of Luca.

His father, that's another story.

"I didn't put her in restraints," Luca says. "I didn't drag her down into the basement cellar. That was Moreno."

My chair squeaks as I stand and come face-to-face with Luca. "But you didn't let her go, either."

"No, I didn't." He breathes heavily, glancing me over, his gaze wandering down my body and then to my lips.

I've seen that heated glare before. If we weren't sleeping in separate rooms, I'd be on my tiptoes and leaning in to kiss him.

But instead, I fold my arms across my chest. "Why?"

"Because she had information!" Luca shouts. "She knew where you were going, at least I thought she did. Kensley definitely knew too much. You're lucky Moreno didn't tell Dante everything."

My breath catches, and I feel my heartbeat quicken. "Moreno kept a secret from Dante?"

"More like kept information. I'm not sure why, don't ask me," Luca gripes. "I would have told my father, but then again, I'd have done anything in my power to piss you off."

Well, it's working.

Nodding, I take a step back and turn with my back to Luca, gathering my notebook and my textbook, putting everything back into my bookbag.

Luca grabs my hips from behind, startling me. His hands grab my arms, pinning me against the table, face down.

I gasp, feeling his hard-on poking me from behind. "I should take you right here, right now, let everyone know you belong to me."

There's no warmth in his words, no glee.

It's pure possession.

My heart stammers, and I try to push Luca away, but he's too strong.

"I'm not fucking you in here," I growl, elbowing him to let me go.

He releases his clutches on me, and I spin around to face him. The edge of my rear is against the table, and he's invading my personal space.

Any other time and I'd be turned on.

To be honest, I'm a little aroused right now, just being in his proximity does that to me, but I'm not about to offer up some sort of hate-fuck to satisfy him.

Not when anyone could walk by or Zeke could climb out of bed and witness his father fucking his mother on the study table.

"Oh, sweetheart, you'll fuck me when and where I tell you," Luca whispers into my ear. "Because we're married."

I roll my eyes and stomp on his toe.

"Ever heard of consent?" I growl at him. "Just because we're married, doesn't mean you get to demand when we have sex. So, go fuck off! You've become exactly like your father!"

SIX

LUCA

Harper knows the exact words to say to rile me up. Like an infection, her words plague me.

"I'm not my father," I growl and step away from her.

She is right, though. I'd never force her to have sex with me.

Marriage.

That's something entirely different. Neither of us had a choice, but I'd never force myself on her.

And I hate myself for nearly losing control, wanting to fuck her senseless and make her beg me to forgive her.

Because that's all it would take to melt away my anger right now. Spending time with her, she gets under my skin, makes me want to forget why I hate her.

Although I'm not sure I can ever truly hate Harper Ricci. After all, she is my *wife*.

The word still feels foreign to me.

Only my closest teammates, the ones who are of mafia blood, know the truth—Liam and Ashton.

Everyone else on the team thinks I'm crazy for marrying Harper. But at least I don't have to worry about us having any house parties. With Zeke under our roof, the partying days at our place are over.

Chase plans on hosting nights that we have a home game. When we win, there will be a party; when we lose, probably a sulkfest. He moved into the old place that I had last semester with our other teammates Rowan, Miles, and Brooks. They're first years, and when they heard from Chase that they could move out of the dorms, they jumped at the opportunity.

After our terse study session, Harper and Liam are on the couch, Ashton and Nova sitting on the floor.

"Let's play a game," Nova says and sips her mocktail. At least I'm assuming that's what she's having, because all the alcohol has been hidden from her.

"What kind of a game?" Ashton asks, but there's definitely hesitation on his behalf.

He's not the only one feeling hesitant, because my little sister's idea of a game isn't something I'd necessarily want to partake in.

"Truth or Dare." Nova is all smiles, and I feel like she's up to no good. She's probably trying to push Harper and me together.

No, thanks.

Harper is not my favorite person at the moment.

I can't believe the nerve, her telling me I'm like my father, and Ashton comes in a rough second, tutoring *my wife*.

I should be over it. Rationally, I know he's not hitting on her. He wouldn't betray me like that, but I still can't help but feel the jealousy building within me when I see the two of them together.

Laughing.

Smiling.

It's not easy being married when secrets keep tearing us apart.

Our relationship isn't built on trust.

Ashton wouldn't know what that's like, how easy he has it right now.

I don't want to feel this way, the burn in my stomach, the ache in my heart, the rage building inside of me with each glance and smile they share.

Their friendship isn't built on lies.

How can I not feel jealous?

Liam stretches his arms on the sofa and smirks. "I could play a game. Not really into the dare part of Truth or Dare. How about we just have to answer whatever's asked of us."

Nova's eyes flicker to Liam. "Chicken." She emits a heavy sigh. "But fine, I could do a game of just truths." It's like they're sharing a secret.

For fuck's sake.

Is everyone keeping secrets from me, or am I just growing more paranoid like my father?

Spending time with him *is* rubbing off on me.

Grumbling, I'm not keen on this little game, but I tolerate it. Spending time, all of us together, is rare these days.

I exhale through my nose, grab a beer from the fridge, and grab a seat on the floor. "Yeah, sure. Hit me with your best shot." I offer to go first, at least just to rip it off like a Band-Aid. The longer they have to think up questions, the tougher it will become.

Ashton smirks. "I'll start. How long are you going to stay angry with me for studying with Harper?"

Maybe I should be reconsidering and opt for a quiet night in my room, in bed.

I roll my eyes and take a swig of my beer. "This would be better as a drinking game," I mutter.

"I'm game!" Nova jumps up from her position on the floor, and I scowl at her.

"There's beer in the fridge. That's all that's in this house," I say.

Liam and Ashton both glare at me. I swear it's the look of *we know you're lying* but neither call me out, either.

It's nice that they're both my teammates and have my back.

"Whatever." Nova rolls her eyes and plops back down.

"My turn," I say and smirk.

Ashton laughs. "The fuck it is. You didn't answer the question."

I sip my beer, pretending I didn't notice. "Oh. Didn't I? Well, as long as you're not hitting on Harper and keeping your grimy paws off her, I think we'll be okay."

Ashton runs a hand through his hair. Frustration marks his forehead, with his vein protruding slightly. "You both realize my intention was just studying?" Ashton glances from Harper to me.

"Of course, it was!" Harper's eyes widen, and I'm surprised she's not screaming in my face. "We're married. Maybe that doesn't mean anything to *you*, Luca, but it means something to me. I'd never cheat on you! Are you always going to be such a caveman? Or is there any chance of you evolving?"

She has a way of trying to get under my skin, but I refuse to let her succeed. "It's not your question, Harper." I shoot a look at her, indicating that I have no plan of answering her.

"Don't worry. It was rhetorical."

My eyebrows narrow as I turn my focus to Ashton. "Why are you suddenly not bringing countless girls to your bedroom?"

I don't dare ask is it because he still has a crush on Harper. It would just be another fight tonight, and I'm growing weary from all our arguing.

Ashton not having sex isn't an option, which means he's been bedding girls in their dorm rooms or apartments. I've got no issues with that, but I've been wondering since before we moved into the new place, why the change?

I hadn't intended to ask, because quite frankly, I know it's none of my business.

But if Ashton is going to be meddling in my relationship, then it's time for me to fucking mess with him.

Ashton presses his lips together, and he's quiet.

A little too quiet.

He runs his fingers over the carpet before he glances up at me. "I asked you first. You don't get to ask me a question next, but since I have nothing to hide, I thought you wouldn't want me to bring *countless girls* into our new place. Seeing as how you have a toddler under your roof."

His answer surprises me.

I nod curtly and glance at Harper, whose gaze is tight on Ashton.

"My question is for Harper," I say, wanting to know why she's looking at him *like that*.

Liam shakes his head, interrupting me. "You've already asked your question. My turn. Someone ask me something, but make it interesting. This truth game is uninspiring."

Nova rolls her eyes at Liam. "That's not how this game works—but whatever. What's the deal with you and Iris?" She's waiting for him to elaborate.

We all are waiting for more details.

"Iris?" I ask. I wasn't aware Liam was dating anyone.

"My friend with benefits." Liam glares at Nova. "How do you know about *her*?"

"You left your phone on the couch the other night, and she texted you. Her messages were on your home screen."

His eyes widen slightly, but he shifts on the sofa. He's trying to play it cool, but I can see the sweat beading on his brow.

"How much did you see?" Liam rubs his hands over his pants.

He's definitely sweating.

"Do you mean read?" Nova smirks. She's toying with him. I know that smile, she's full of shit and he's buying it.

"Don't harass him," I growl at my little sister. "He's allowed some privacy."

Nova snorts. "Sure. Whatever."

Liam glares at Nova. "What about you? Do you want to tell everyone who *you're dating?*"

Nova clears her throat and pulls her knees to her

chest. "I'm not dating anyone." Her voice crackles as it catches in her throat.

I'd know if Nova had a boyfriend.

She'd be on her phone all the time, texting him if such a boy existed.

If Liam is trying to make her feel small, pitiful for not having anyone show interest in her, I'm not going to have it. "Nova's too smart to get wrapped up in a relationship. She's focusing on her studies. Unlike some people." I glare at Liam to shut him up.

Nova grabs her mocktail and stands. "I'm bored. This game isn't any fun. I'm going to go read in my room."

She's pretending not to be hurt.

I let her go. It's better if the game ends before any more damage is done. I stand, not wanting to get stuck answering anything more about Harper or her and Ashton studying. I'm still steamed about it, even though I don't want to be.

I can't help my feelings.

I catch a few hours of sleep, but after fighting with Harper when trying to help her study and that ridiculous truth game I never should have agreed to, I'm not the least bit tired.

I'm overstimulated.

I wake before the sun rises, which isn't a surprise since practice always starts at six-thirty sharp. We do warmups on the ice and drills.

At least the ice arena gives me purpose, and maybe it can help clear my head.

"How's married life?" Chase skates alongside me as we work on our passes and then shooting into the goal.

"Fucking wonderful," I say.

"Trouble in paradise already?" Rowan overhears us.

Fuck.

I need to play it cool. These guys don't have an inkling of what's going on between us, why we got hitched, or that my family is mafia.

Asking questions will just get all of us into trouble. I'm not an idiot. I know that Ashton has been spying for Dante. I'm just not sure if I'm his target or Harper.

Possibly both of us.

"She wanted a honeymoon," I say. It's an easy and believable lie.

"Don't they all?" Chase quips. "Take her somewhere for spring break."

His suggestion wouldn't be bad if I didn't want to spend another moment in the same room as Harper.

I skate off, avoiding any more discussion of my *wife*. Maybe I should have pretended that we didn't get married, but the ring on my finger is a blatant reminder that it happened.

We finish drills, shower, and the team grabs breakfast together in the dining hall.

I'm starving, and Ashton grabs a seat next to me. I swear he's trying to make sure that I don't crack under pressure, and not from hockey.

"I can't believe you didn't invite us to the wedding," Rowan says as he gestures at the ring on my finger. "When did that happen?"

"Saturday," I say, between bites of eggs. "It was a very small ceremony."

Not a complete lie, since when we did exchange vows, there were only a few people present. It wasn't the wedding Mom had planned for us. It wasn't the wedding day I envisioned either, chasing down my bride.

"Is the wife going to be at Thursday's game?" Brooks asks. He's the least annoying of the freshmen who are interrogating me about the wedding, probably because he hasn't met Harper yet.

"Harper?" I say and take another bite of breakfast. "Doubt it. She has a kid, early bedtime and all that." It's an easy excuse that I can use, and since we're playing an away game, I don't have to lie.

"Your kid?" Brooks asks, his eyes widening.

"Only by marriage," I say and pause, rubbing the back of my neck. That's a conversation that we never had. If something does happen to Harper, who gets custody of Zeke?

A heavy conversation that I don't ever want to think about, so I push that thought aside.

"Damn. Marriage and a kid," Rowan says. "You really signed up for the entire package."

Ashton grins. "Harper is the entire package. Have you seen her? Curves and all." He makes a chef's kiss gesture, and I want to fucking end him.

I glare at Ashton. If he's trying to help, it's not working. All he's doing is making me jealous the way he speaks about *my wife.*

Ashton notices my discomfort and forces a smile. "I'm just saying congrats, man. You got the best of both worlds."

No, I got a raw deal, but I can't gripe about it to my teammates.

Liam sits across from me. He's silent, scrolling through his phone and eating his breakfast, keeping to himself. I appreciate him not making things worse for me.

He knows the truth, just like Ashton. But Ashton would rather give me shit.

"Anything interesting?" I say, glancing at Liam, hoping to steer the conversation away from my fucked-up love life.

Liam smiles and shakes his head. "Just my friend with benefits," he says. "She likes to send me pictures."

Rowan reaches for Liam's phone, and he snarls at him, shoving him off. "Get your own girlfriend."

"Wow," Rowan says. "I didn't think you'd be so possessive since she's just your side piece."

"She's actually a friend. We just hook up when we're both in town. They're pictures of her and her dog, jackass," Liam growls at him.

Liam's friends with benefits doesn't go to school at Evergreen University, which makes the benefits situation seem less than ideal. But I know better than to mock Liam. He'd just pick a fight with me, and I already have Ashton doing that enough as it is.

"Would be better if they were pictures of her and her cat," Ashton snickers.

"Do you have a death wish, Rinaldi?" Liam glares down at Ashton and then throws a croissant at his face.

"Oh, he definitely has one," I say as I take another bite of my breakfast.

Ashton steals the pastry that assaulted him. "Thanks, man." He holds the sweet treat up and grins before taking a bite.

The crowd at the ice arena is covered in green and black. We're playing the Predators tonight, a team that's only a few hours from the city. It's a smaller private college, but they've been our longest and biggest rival.

Liam is stoked since his friend with benefits attends Great Falls College. We'd usually drive home after a game that's within a couple of hours' commute, but the forecast is calling for several inches of snow overnight, and it started after we arrived.

Coach booked a block of rooms for us at the local hotel in town. I share with Ashton, who isn't the worst roommate to have, although whoever gets Liam is lucky, since he won't be staying at the hotel.

There are no rules about leaving. If you have family, you're allowed to crash with them for the night, so long as you're back on the bus in the morning when we leave. Otherwise, you better find your own ride back to campus.

"The place is packed," I say, noting the crowd. There's a handful of Narwhals fans that stand out in teal and white, but there aren't too many in the arena. I suspect the weather kept a lot of our fans from coming out tonight.

We warm up on the ice, do some stretching, and get ready to annihilate the Predators. There are no other options.

We need a win tonight.

Liam is on one side of me, Ashton on the other. "Did you see who is in the stands tonight?" Liam nods toward the plexiglass.

My vision scans the crowd, wondering who Liam sees.

In the front row, a gentleman with thick dark hair and even darker eyes is wearing a business suit. He seems a bit out of place, but I recognize him. "Is that—"

"Kyler Greyson," Liam says, and his jaw clenches. "His annoying brat, Bristol, attends Great Falls."

My breath catches in my throat. "You know Greyson?"

"Which one—yes." Liam answers a little too quickly. "Not that well. We went to private school together since we were little."

"I meant Kyler Greyson." I don't care about Bristol. "Any chance of an introduction?" I ask, skating backward as my gaze doesn't leave Mr. Greyson's.

"Only if you want to make it yourself," Liam says.

Greyson is the one chance I have at making the NHL and getting away from my father.

That's not to say I couldn't be drafted if I enroll in the NHL draft, but it's a long shot. There are better players at other schools. I may be the best at Evergreen, but I'm not the best out there.

I'm not arrogant enough to think I have a future secured in playing professional hockey.

"Better make a good impression." Ashton smacks my back.

He knows what I'm up against—my own father.

It's the mafia or hockey.

Technically, Dante told me after a professional hockey career, I would still be required to join the family business, but if I make it big, there's no way he'll have a lick of control over me.

I just have to get famous.

Which starts with impressing Kyler Greyson, the new owner of the Ice Dragons and former NHL star hockey player.

"Or you could cozy up to Bristol and get me that introduction." I wiggle my eyebrows at him.

Liam snorts. He stretches on the ice, getting loosened up before our game. "You've clearly never met Bristol."

"What about Brooks? Is he dating anyone?" Look at me, trying to play matchmaker, so I get an introduction to Kyler Greyson.

"You'd have to ask Brooks." Liam rolls his eyes and skates away from me. "But I wouldn't do that to a friend," he shouts.

During the first quarter, I try to focus on the game and not on the fact Kyler is watching us play. He's probably more focused on the Predators than the

Narwhals. The only way I have a chance of meeting with him is if I'm impressive in tonight's match.

I manage to make two scores early in the first period. The Predators don't seem to be taking the match seriously, but then I get bodychecked when chasing after the puck and my helmet flies off.

Fucking asshole.

"Think you're some hotshot," Tucker taunts. He doesn't back down, his fist meeting my jaw, and it stings.

Ashton is right behind me, grabbing the jersey of the guy who hit me and slinging him around on the ice, throwing punch after punch into his side.

The other team races after Ashton. Brooks and Rowan move in to defend.

The referee blows his whistle, not that anyone can hear it.

I'm yanked back by an unfamiliar set of arms, and the fight breaks apart as we're separated. At least Tucker is thrown into the penalty box.

Liam glances me over. "You okay?" His gaze lands on my jaw for a moment longer than necessary.

I'll definitely be sporting a bruise tomorrow.

"Fine."

Tucker seems to have it out for me for the rest of the night. I'm not sure, but it feels like the entire Predators team is in on his little game of beat the shit out of me.

Every time I have the puck, they chase me. Yes, that's how the game is supposed to go, but after I shoot it to Ashton or Chase, they still faceplant me against the glass.

Every fucking time.

Tucker is the first to attack me. Then it's one of his buddies, either Black or Wells. They play dirty.

The first time, at least Tucker landed in the penalty box. The second and third times, I get thrown in too.

For fuck's sake, I can't catch a break.

That's just the first period.

In the second period, I feel off my game. Probably because I'm getting the shit kicked out of me every two minutes.

It's fight after fight, which isn't a huge surprise except they keep jumping me. And some of the body checking is legitimate, but it's the shit where they intentionally grab my jersey or my stick and restrain me that should result in a penalty for holding.

But the referees don't notice or at least they're not calling the penalties.

It's like they look the other way when there's misconduct on the Predators' side, but we so much as sneeze in their direction and we're getting thrown in the penalty box.

It's any wonder our team is still ahead, but the Predators are closing the gap, and by the end of the second period, we're tied.

We skate off the ice to the locker room during intermission, and I'm sweating my ass off. My cheek stings, as does my jaw, but I ignore it, pumped up on adrenaline.

Coach goes over a few plays that we made earlier and what we can do to tighten our game. "They're playing dirty. Don't let them get into your heads."

Too late for that.

I don't even know why they're riling me up so much, but it's working. Probably because I'm already tense and frustrated with all the shit going on in my day-to-day life. Between Harper and Dante, I'm drowning in irritation and annoyance.

Tucker is just the final straw, it seems.

"Get back out there. You guys can still clinch this win in the third period. Give it all you've got."

Coach continues yammering on, but I drown it out. I fix the laces on my skates and head back out with the team for our final period.

Ashton scores a goal in the last two minutes, and Tucker comes by, stealing the puck, sending it to his buddy Wells and they score, tying the game up.

It's too close, and I don't want their team getting an ounce of victory tonight. It should be ours. In the final seconds of the game, I score, securing our win, and it feels amazing.

I want to celebrate with the team and our friends.

After we shower and clean up, we head to the hotel. There's alcohol snuck in by one of the seniors, since most of us aren't old enough to drink.

A half dozen of the guys hang out in Ashton's and my room, celebrating our win.

Liam hangs out with us for an hour until he gets his booty call and hurries out to meet up with her.

"Has anyone ever met Liam's special friend?" I want to know if this girl actually exists or if he is harboring some other illicit secret.

Ashton shrugs. "Can't say that I have. But didn't he have pictures of her on his phone?"

"No one ever saw what they actually looked like. He wouldn't show us." Rowan stretches out on my bed, making himself at home.

"We should sneak out and follow him." Brooks doesn't so much as budge from his seat on the sofa. He points at the door. "Who's with me?"

My legs don't feel capable of moving. I collapse onto my bed and shove Rowan over. "You're hogging half my bed. I don't share with anyone."

"Not even your wife?" Rowan raises an eyebrow.

I shut my eyes, sigh, and then open them as I reach for my beer. I'm going to need something stronger if we're talking about Harper.

"Going that well, huh?" Brooks stretches his legs in front of him and then cracks his neck from side to side.

"Everything is fine." I lie and hope I can go back to my uncanny acting ability that we're happily in love.

But I don't feel like putting on a show tonight. I already had my ass kicked on the ice, and while we won, I can't help but feel a tiny bit defeated.

"What about you?" Rowan turns to Ashton, who is seated on his bed by himself.

"We're not discussing my love life." Ashton's eyes widen as he takes a swig from his beer.

Who the hell is Ashton Rinaldi dating? I haven't seen any girl climb into his bed since we moved into the new place. Besides, he doesn't date. He's more of a one-night stand guy.

"Because Ashton doesn't have a love life." I point at him, waiting for him to tell the guys that they're wrong, that he doesn't believe in dating and love.

Ashton falls silent and takes another drink from his beer bottle. He tips his head back, guzzling that fucker right down.

"Who the hell are you dating?" I sit up and glare at him. "I'd know if you brought a girl into our home."

"Relax." Ashton puts the bottle down on the nightstand. "It's just me and my hand."

Brooks snorts with laughter, his face turning bright red.

Rowan shakes his head, grinning like an idiot. "If you're that hard up, there are puck bunnies who'd give you a hand—or a mouth."

Ashton stands, takes his phone with him, and heads toward the bathroom. "You guys are assholes." He slams the bathroom door shut behind himself.

SEVEN

ASHTON

I can't believe I let the guys harass me. I could have used any number of comebacks. It's not like I have no wit.

But when it comes to Nova, I have to keep her a secret.

The worst part is everyone on the team knows about Nova and me.

Everyone except my best friend, Luca.

They're keeping my secret, for now, but it's clear they may not keep it much longer.

Rowan even bringing up the question about who I'm dating is such a shit thing to do. He was there the night of the party when I hooked up with Nova for the first time.

All of the team was there, even Luca. But Luca just happened to be too preoccupied with Harper upstairs to know what we were doing downstairs and then later in my bedroom.

I flip the fan on in the bathroom, giving me a little privacy before I sit on the edge of the bathtub. Glancing at my phone, I video call Nova.

Her eyes light up when she answers the call. "Hey, stranger!"

Her voice is music to my soul. But seeing her smile, she manages to erase all the fears and doubts I have about the two of us dating.

"Hey, we won." I smile, the flood of endorphins not entirely passed through my system yet. The beer also helps, gives me an added boost of confidence. Not that I need it. "I miss you."

"You always miss me." Nova's nose scrunches and she blows me a kiss. "Did you score tonight?"

"Only in hockey." I wink at her, because she's the only girl I have eyes for. I used to like taking a new girl to bed after every party, but there's something about Nova that changes my needs.

Or maybe it's just the fact that I want her, and I worry someone else might steal her away if I don't lock her down with fantastic sex at every opportunity.

She stares at me and smiles through the video call. "You are something else. Where are you? It looks like a bathroom in the background."

Grimacing, I realize that being on video probably wasn't ideal, but I wanted to see her face, hear her voice, stare into her sapphire gaze.

"Yeah, the guys were just asking if I have a girlfriend. I couldn't get away fast enough."

"Wow." Nova laughs and brings a hand up to her lips to keep her voice down. "So, what did you tell them?"

"Nothing. I couldn't mention you, and I wasn't going to lie."

Nova smirks. "So, you ran to the bathroom to hide?" She's teasing me, but I'm keeping the secret for her sake too. Luca isn't going to be happy when he finds out I'm dating his little sister.

Well, he'll probably be angrier at me.

Either way, there's no good outcome in this situation for me. I can't imagine him throwing his arm around me and telling me to have fun.

"I came into the bathroom to call you." It's a half-truth, but Nova has the ability to see right through me.

"You ran and hid. But it's okay, I like the benefit of you and me getting to talk alone. Are you sharing a room with my brother?"

I sigh. "Yes." Another reason the bathroom was the safest place to talk to Nova. It's not like I can have a private conversation in the hotel room, especially when Luca doesn't know I'm dating anyone.

"It's just one night. Don't sound so bummed."

"I'm not. I just miss you." I like being able to sneak across the hallway and cuddle with Nova, climb into her bed and wrap my arms around her. I don't get to do that on nights when we are away. "What are you wearing?"

Nova grins and glances down at her pajama shirt. "Nothing."

"Sweetheart, I can see your clothes."

She rolls her eyes and then slowly draws the phone downward so I can see everything she's wearing. She's got a cute matching pajama outfit with penguins. It's a shorts set and rides up at her hips at just the right angle.

"Do you want to do that again? But slower and spread your legs for me."

Nova's eyes widen. "Are you trying to have phone sex with me?" Her voice squeaks, and her nervousness is actually quite sweet.

A virgin in phone sex.

"I was hoping we might be able to indulge each other in a little fantasy phone play."

Her eyes are wide, and she hangs up on me.

It's clear she clicked the end call, and it wasn't a mistake or the phone call being dropped because of the weather.

I shoot her a text.

So, I guess that's a no.

She calls me back, but this time there's no video call, just a plain old boring phone conversation.

"Hey," I whisper, glad that she's not ignoring me.

"I'm not ready for phone sex. I mean, it involves a lot of talking and describing, and I'm nervous to do that."

"You don't have to be nervous around me. It's not like I've had tons of phone sex." The number of times I can count on one hand—well, more like one finger. Phone sex isn't a high priority when you're with a different girl each time.

"I like you, Ashton."

I can't help but smile. "In case you haven't noticed, I like you too, Nova. I could do the dirty talking, and you could just listen. Touch yourself for me. Let me hear your soft whimpers that turn me on so much, baby."

There's a soft gasp in her voice.

I smile. "Yes, just like that. But you don't have to if you're not comfortable. If you say no, I'll respect your decision."

"Tell me what you'd do to me," Nova rasps, and I can hear her shifting on the mattress.

I wish that we still had a video call happening, but I'll take what I can get with her.

My eyes close for a moment and I realize I, too, need to get more comfortable. The edge of the bathtub isn't doing it for me. I grab the box of tissues, toss it on the floor, and move to sit on the ground, my back against the wall, the bath rug beneath me as I stretch my legs out.

"First, I'd kiss a trail of soft kisses across your collarbone. I know how much you like it when I kiss your neck. My tongue would tease that little spot that makes your hips gyrate against me."

She hums softly; it's a slight, subtle moan, and it's enough to make my cock twitch in my jeans.

"What else?" she asks.

There's movement on her end, and I can't help but smile. "Take off your clothes for me," I command.

"Is this you telling me you want them off or you actually want them off?" Her question is so innocent it's adorable.

"I want your clothes fucking off, sweetheart," I growl.

There's a soft rustling on her end. I presume she's disrobing, and I wait a few moments for her to finish. "Tell me when you're naked and under the covers."

"Already there," Nova says, matter-of-fact. "Keep going."

I chuckle at her eagerness and dip my head back against the wall. "I want your hands to explore your body. Let your fingers glide across your chest but just tease your nipple. It's my lips doing that, my mouth on your skin. I go slowly at first, watching as your chest rises and falls, listening to the sweet moans that spill from your lips before my tongue circles your nipple."

"Ashton." Her words purr out of her, and it sounds like heaven.

"I love it when you moan my name." I run a hand over my jeans, my palms sweaty. The bathroom is already stifling.

Each breath is a soft pant, and I bite my bottom lip to keep some semblance of control. Fuck, she turns me on so damn much.

"What next?" Nova asks, her sweet, innocent voice giving me a raging hard-on.

I breathe in deeply and sharply, trying to regain my composure. I cannot come yet. She hasn't even had one orgasm, let alone multiples.

Nova is the only woman who knows how to make me both so strong and so incredibly weak at the same time. She is my undoing.

I blink through the foggy haze. "Let your fingers skim across your stomach and down lower, but don't touch yourself just yet."

"Okay."

A smile splays across my face. Gosh, I really wish she was on video for this call. Maybe next time, I can convince her to turn her camera back on so I can watch her touch herself.

"My lips caress your skin." My own breathing deepens as the air grows thicker, hotter. "My mouth kisses lightly up your thighs, toward your arousal."

Nova's breath catches with a gasp, and my heart flutters at the sweet sounds that she makes.

They're such a fucking turn-on. "Do you want me to taste you tonight?"

"Yes." Nova moans, and I take that as encouragement to continue.

"You sound so fucking sexy. I spread your legs wider, put one leg over each shoulder as I run my tongue along your slit."

"Fuck."

The smile spreads across my face. "Are you touching yourself, sweetheart?"

"Maybe?" Her voice catches in her throat.

"Sit on your hands."

"What?" There's concern in her tone.

"I didn't tell you to touch your pussy, yet. Sit on your hands; punish yourself for me."

Nova whimpers, and my cock strains for release. I'm throbbing, and I can only imagine Nova feels the same way.

"Are you being a good girl and doing as I've told you?" I wait for her to answer me.

"Yes."

I unzip my jeans and unbutton the top, pulling my cock out. "I'm so hard for you. I'm touching myself, but you have to wait. You have to listen to me stroke my cock."

There's a bit of precum at the tip, and I use it as lube. "If you had the video on, I'd show you how hard I am for you. My cock is dripping to be inside you."

Another whimper from her and I'm teetering toward an abyss of pure oblivion, but I'm not ready to go there yet, not ready to make that jump into sweet ecstasy.

"You can move your hands out from beneath your bottom, but only trace along your pussy. Don't touch yourself fully yet."

Her soft gasps grow more pronounced. "Are you wet for me?"

"Yes."

"Good. I'm glad I make you wet. I wish I could taste your sweetness. My tongue would be all over that sexy pussy, and I'd lick you in long, slow motions, working you up into a frenzy."

"I'm already there," Nova whispers. "You're making me ache so much."

The smile spreads across my face. What I wouldn't give to feel that throbbing around my cock.

"It's a good kind of ache, isn't it, sweetheart?"

"Yes." She's breathier, more relaxed, and hell, sounding sexier if that's even possible. "I want your cock in me."

"You don't want my tongue on your clit? Because I want to feel you rock those gorgeous hips against my face."

"Ashton." Her moan is delicious, and I don't feel deserving enough to hear her, but I desire more.

"Move your hips against the mattress. Touch yourself for me." I crave her body, her heart, her mind. I want all of her.

There are soft movements in the background, and I can only envision she's doing as I've told her. "I want your cock inside of me."

"Fuck, baby. I want that too," I rasp. Her words make my shaft throb. I stroke myself, imagining it is her hand, her lips, her head bobbing up and down, taking me deeper.

Her moans grow more pronounced, sexier, as she nears the edge. "Come for me," I whisper, finding it more of a struggle to speak, to form coherent thoughts as my cock aches for her pussy.

She whimpers and moans. "I'm so close, please, Ashton." Her voice begs for me to fuck her, and I swear if I could get to her safely tonight, I would.

"You're doing so good, baby." My voice is hardly above a whisper. "I love watching and hearing you come."

Nova moans, her gasps growing more audible as I listen to her chase her orgasm. It's everything I could have imagined and even better.

After, she's panting hard, breathing heavily as she seems to settle down. "Did you come?" Nova asks.

"Not yet." My voice is gravelly. I stroke my cock, head tipped back, my motions faster with my fist. Now that I know she's reached her climax, I allow myself to hurry mine.

"Come for me, Ashton." Nova's words echo in my ear. "I want to taste you in my mouth."

Her naughty words send me over the edge. My heart pounds wildly, and I tremble, feeling the swell overtake me. I reach for a tissue, spilling my seed into it. I bite down on my bottom lip to keep from moaning out loud. I want Nova to hear me, but I have to be careful. I'm not the only one in this hotel room.

I swear my heart is going to leap out of my chest as my eyes struggle to open. I'm sated, but it was worth it.

Holy fuck, that was good. "Thank you for playing along with me tonight."

Nova initiates the video chat once again, and I click accept.

She's lying in bed curled up on her side, the lights out, but I can catch a faint glow from her phone. "You were right, phone sex is fun."

I wish I could be curled up against her, but staring at her will have to be enough. "Video sex will be even better the next time."

Nova smiles and glances away. "No promises, but if you want to be on video while I have my camera off, I won't say no."

EIGHT

LIAM

As soon as I get the text from Iris, I'm racing across campus at lightning speed. While we're just friends with benefits, I look forward to spending time together.

It doesn't hurt that she's been sending me nudes.

She's also sent me photos of her and the shelter dogs that she's been cuddling. It's part of her work-study that she's doing at Great Falls.

I swear if she weren't living in the dorms, she'd probably have adopted all of them.

I head up to her dorm room and give a prominent knock, waiting for her to let me in.

"Just a second!" a female voice shouts over the loud music. I'm surprised anyone could even hear me knocking.

Bristol Greyson yanks open the door, stares back at me, her eyes glower and she slams it shut.

What the hell?

Does Iris know Bristol? Are they new roommates?

I fucking hate Bristol Greyson. She's a spoiled rich kid whose dad used to play in the NHL and then bought the team.

He's a billionaire.

Hell, I read that he was a billionaire before he even played hockey, which makes sense. No hockey players are rolling in that kind of dough. He did some stocks or bonds or something financial when he was young. Hit big. Made lots of money.

He's a rich guy with a snotty daughter.

She was a brat in the first grade, when we were

forced into the same class, and a hellraiser in middle school.

We both went to the same private school growing up. By high school, we were in different social circles.

I don't want to admit that she actually turned from ugly duckling into a real beauty. Doesn't matter how hot she is, she's dripping with venom.

The girl has serious claws and teeth that bite.

I pound on the door again, and Bristol throws it open, glares at me, grabs me by the arm, and yanks me into her room before slamming the door shut.

"What. The. Hell." I glare at her and glance around.

She turns the music down on her speakers.

Where the fuck is Iris?

This isn't Iris's room. Was there a change in her dorm? Am I on the wrong fucking floor?

"Is this 416?" I glance around because I'd recognize Iris's room with her puppy posters littered all over her walls.

There are no puppy posters.

This room has a darker overtone. While the walls are painted a standard gray, they have smaller posters with a gothic vibe. There's some witchy shit going on here.

"Voodoo Queen." I glare at Bristol.

She rolls her eyes. "You always were overdramatic. What the hell do you want?"

"I'm looking for Iris. Room 416."

"You're on the wrong floor, dumbass." Bristol blocks me from leaving, a wicked smile on her face.

My phone buzzes, and I retrieve it from my pocket, glancing at Iris sending me a text.

Waiting. ETA?

"My mistake. I wouldn't want to bother you." I gesture to the door behind her, and she cackles.

It's one of those unmistakable witchy cackles. Oh gosh, the girl is going to put a spell on me. Or maybe it's a hex or curse. Is there really any difference?

"Girlfriend?" Bristol guesses. She looks amused, eyeing me up and down. "I saw you play tonight. You weren't—bad." She really knows how to get under my skin.

"I kicked ass on the ice." I glare at her, stepping closer. She can't intimidate me like she did when we were six.

I'm not claiming to be a saint. Sure, I picked on her, but she was a rich kid. It wasn't anything she didn't deserve.

My twin sister and I were only enrolled because of our biological father, whom we didn't even know until we were four. Getting thrown into a new home, new school, new family, it was wild and turbulent.

I had a few rebellious years early on, when I met the brat who stands in front of me, but she continued to torment me at any chance she had.

And, of course, I fought back.

It's what we Morettis do.

"You think you played good tonight?" Bristol folds her arms across her chest, her Predators jersey rising up slightly as she argues with me.

The creamy skin of her stomach and her freckles call out to me.

Fuck no.

I glance away.

She snorts and throws her hands up in the air. “See, can’t even look at me. You know I’m right. You played worth shit.”

“I scored a goal.”

“One measly goal.” Bristol meets my gaze. “Your teammate is a better hockey player than you.”

I invade her personal space, my arm coming up against the door, blocking her in, keeping her within my grasp.

“Say that again,” I growl at her.

Bristol stares up at me, her gaze not the least bit wavering. “You’re a shitty hockey player. Your teammate Ricci, he knows how to fucking score. You should take lessons from him. Maybe he’ll teach you how to hold your stick and—”

I lean down and bite her lips. My heart pounds wildly out of control.

Her body pauses for a brief moment before she succumbs, wrapping her fingers in my hair. The kiss deepens, her lips part, and I'm pushing my tongue inside of her mouth, exploring her in a wave of unrelenting passion.

With one hand on her waist and the other against the door, I pull her closer, tighter against me.

Bristol's hands move from my hair down to my waist. She manages to spin us around, her tongue sliding across mine, and fuck, her fingers are digging into my hips, clawing at me.

She's a beast. Had I known, I'd have kissed her years ago.

Swiftly and expertly, she opens the door, shoving me out into the hallway. "You have to go."

Her lips are swollen, her breathing ragged.

I'm not sure how I even ended up out in the hallway, gasping, my heart thumping against my ribcage as she slams the door in my face.

My phone buzzes again. I ignore it. "Bristol." I don't knock, but I know she can hear me. She must hear me because she has to be thinking about *that kiss.*

She doesn't answer.

I huff and walk down the hallway, as if I'm doing the walk of shame. I head for the elevator and glance at my phone—another text from Iris.

You still coming?

After what just happened between Bristol and me, I can't.

I have to end things between us.

It feels wrong. And not because I haven't kissed two girls in one night, although usually they're in my bed.

It's Bristol.

And she's put me under some crazy spell, because everything I've ever experienced is pale compared to the feel of her lips sizzling on mine.

She's a fucking witch, and I want more.

NINE

HARPER

I'm dreading the entire drive to the Ricci family's home. Tomorrow, we're scheduled to take pictures for our wedding, and instead of coming on Saturday, our presence was requested Friday evening.

While I knew Luca would be expected to arrive on Friday and stay through Sunday morning, I wasn't expecting Zeke and myself to both have to stay the weekend too.

Can't say I'm happy with the news.

Zeke is asleep in the backseat.

"I heard you guys won the game yesterday." I glance at Luca, who has his attention firmly planted on the road. He's sporting a bruise on his chin that he didn't have yesterday morning. "What happened?" I gesture toward the blemish.

"Hazard of the job." He glances at me. "Hockey, not mafia."

If he's trying to make a joke, there's no smile or laughter adorning his face. "I didn't figure your father was behind the bruise. Rough game?"

"I kept getting my face smacked into the plexiglass. Wasn't my night."

"But you won. That has to count for something."

He sighs. "Yeah, I scored three goals too."

"Three?" My eyes widen. "That's great!"

He purses his lips, clearly something else seems to be on his mind.

I refrain from asking because I already know he's not going to tell me. It seems we're not sharing much lately, aside from a last name.

Luca glances in the backseat, and then his shoulders soften. "Zeke seems to be doing better."

Smiling, I nod. "Yeah, I should probably thank your mom for making that call to the pediatrician, bringing him out on such short notice."

He shifts and glances at me. "Do you think you'll ever want any more kids?"

His question catches me off guard. "Yeah, maybe. I mean, I'd like to give Zeke a sibling. One who's close in age would be great, but I don't think either one of us are ready for that kind of commitment."

His gaze tightens.

"Did I say something wrong?"

Luca shakes his head but doesn't answer.

"Clearly, I did. You don't look happy with my response." I shift in my seat, turning slightly to face him. I hate that he picks now to fight with me while driving. Or maybe it's me who is picking a fight with him. Luca keeps avoiding me, it seems.

Silence fills the void between us.

"Dammit, Luca! I'd rather you fight with me than give me the silent treatment."

"I'm not giving you the silent treatment." He shoots a glance at me. "I'm driving, and fighting isn't going to help us when we have to deal with my parents this evening or pictures tomorrow."

"What will help us?" I ask, waiting for him to tell me how we can fix this mess.

"I don't know." There's an honesty in his words, a conviction that he is at as much a loss as I am.

Luca turns up the radio, deciding we've had enough discussion or lack thereof, and fills the silence in the car.

As we pull up to his parents' house, Zeke begins to stir awake. A few snowflakes begin to fall but the weather report isn't calling for much and the snow that fell last night has already been cleaned up. The roads were clear, but the snow hadn't yet melted.

I unbuckle Zeke from the backseat, and Luca carries our weekend bags inside. There are two bags, one for Luca and one that I'm sharing with Zeke. Although I swear most of the bag is Zeke's, with extra changes of clothes, diapers, and wipes.

Zeke babbles as I carry him out of the cold and into their foyer. Luca removes his own coat and shoes in one swift motion and leaves the bags on the floor inside the door. He helps me remove Zeke's winter gear and shoes before taking him so that I can remove my own coat and shoes.

"I thought I heard you guys," Nikki says, coming toward us. She holds out her hands for Zeke and Luca hands my son over to his grandmother.

"We're going to have so much fun, just the two of us." Nikki drops featherlight kisses on his cheeks and nose.

Zeke squirms but pinches at her cheeks, clearly enjoying the attention.

Nikki heads with him down the hall, and I'm quick to follow after my son. "Where are you taking him?" It's not that I don't trust her. Actually, it is one hundred percent that she is the wife of a mafia don. I don't trust any of them, except Luca.

I want to trust Nikki, especially since she seems to be enthralled with my son. I can't tell if it's the fact she likes babies or that this is her new grandson.

"Do you want to see your new playroom?" Nikki cuddles Zeke and carries him down the hallway. To the left is an open door, and she wanders inside.

I'm right on her heels.

Luca is a few paces behind me. He doesn't seem nearly as concerned, but Zeke is *my* son.

I step in behind Nikki, and the room is covered in toys. They're not all new toys. Against the walls is a white bookshelf, stocked with everything from dolls to race cars. "I had Moreno bring down the kids' toys from the attic."

"You kept our old stuff?" Luca wanders into the playroom, taking all of it in, his gaze moving over the entire room.

"We didn't keep everything, but there were some toys that never got donated and got put away. Yours and Nova's favorites." Nikki brings Zeke over to the child-sized table and puts him down.

His head turns in every direction as he spins around, taking everything in. He runs over to the play kitchen and starts pulling all of the plastic food out.

"That was one of your favorite toys too," Nikki muses.

"Thank you." I'm shocked that Luca's family arranged to have a room devoted to Zeke. He's my son, and while through marriage he's their grandson, he's not theirs by blood.

Luca strolls to the far corner where there's a child's tent set up, the perfect hiding place, it's practically a fortress for a little kid. He bends down, glancing inside. "I always remembered this to be so much bigger. Nova and I used to hide in here for hours."

Nikki smiles faintly, reminiscing. "Yes, I remember that."

"Did you know it was the only place I felt safe?" Luca turns and faces his mother, the smile devoid of warmth. "After what Dante did, it was the one place I knew no one could see me."

Because there weren't any cameras inside the fort, no surveillance. I glance up at the corner of the room and there's a camera with a red flashing light recording us, always watching us.

Nikki pats Luca's arm. "Let's not recount the past." She forces a smile and bends down to Zeke's level.

"I'm glad you like the toys. I hope you'll like your new bedroom."

"Bedroom?" The air leaves my lungs.

Nikki stands, glancing from Zeke to me. "You didn't think we'd have your son sleeping in your bed or the guest room, did you?"

Actually, that's precisely what I expected. It's not like I intend to stay here very often. For one or two nights, Zeke could share a bed with me. That's pretty much what's happened since the wedding. Luca and I haven't slept in the same room, and because I'm sharing a room with Zeke, he keeps climbing into my bed anyhow.

Luca studies my face before glancing at Nikki. "Mom, that really isn't necessary."

"It's already done." Nikki gestures for me to follow her.

I bend down to carry Zeke, and he protests.

"It's okay, you can leave him in here. The room's been babyproofed." Nikki gestures at the walls. "The outlets have been plugged, and the toys are all age-appropriate. Anything too mature is on a higher shelf that he shouldn't be able to reach."

She's truly thought of everything.

I'm reluctant to leave Zeke alone in this place.

Luca senses my hesitation and rests a hand on my back. "I'll stay with Zeke. Mom can show you his room and then later you can show me when I take our things upstairs."

"All right." I exhale a heavy sigh and agree to follow Nikki upstairs. I glance over my shoulder as Zeke hands Luca a toy banana. Luca bends down, taking it from him and pretending to gobble it up, getting a laugh from my little boy.

Nikki leads me upstairs. Beside Luca's room, she opens the door and shows me the child's bedroom that's been carefully put together for Zeke. There's a toddler bed, like the one he has at home against the wall near the window. On the opposite side is a dresser and desk.

There's a stack of toys in the corner of the room and a handful of plush stuffies on the bed.

Nikki wanders over to the dozen or so books cradled in a basket. "Everything in here is new. The books, the stuffed animals—we wanted Zeke to feel at home when he comes to visit."

"That is very kind of you." But all I can keep thinking about is that little boy who was locked in their basement, kidnapped and taken from his family.

Luca had told me that there was no sign of the child. He'd been down in the basement when he'd questioned Kensley. The boy was gone.

But where had he been taken?

There wasn't a damn thing I could do about the missing child, the one Dante had abducted, but I could protect my own son.

"I should get back downstairs and check on the boys." I force a smile.

Nikki reaches for my arm. "I know this isn't what you were expecting when you would one day get married, but we're all trying to accept you and your son. Please don't hurt *my* son."

It's too late for that.

Luca already hates me.

Dinner is rather uneventful. Moreno and Paige join us, but Nova is on campus, and I've never missed her company more.

Of course, Ashton is there with her, which gives them the place almost to themselves. It's not as though Liam cares about Ashton and Nova hooking up.

Luca carries our bags upstairs while I show him Zeke's new bedroom next door to ours.

"At least it's close." He places the bag on Zeke's dresser before heading to our room.

I sift through everything in the weekend bag, grabbing a new diaper for Zeke along with his pajamas.

By the time I get Zeke tucked into bed, read him a story, and get him to sleep, I'm exhausted. I'm reluctant to leave him alone, but there's no bed for me.

I sit on the floor, stretching out, leaning with my back against the wall.

It's not comfortable, and I'm tired, but Zeke is my

everything, and I don't trust Dante or the men who work for him.

I should have grabbed a pillow and blanket, at least I could have slept on the floor.

The house is eerily quiet.

There are no strange sounds, no child whimpering like the first time I'd spent the night months ago.

My body relaxes, and I begin to drift into an unpleasant sleep. My neck throbs even in slumber, and my dreams are of being chased through the forest, carrying Zeke, running for our lives.

I'm startled awake, strong arms beneath me, carrying me as I'm gasping for breath.

My eyes flash open, and Luca's staring back at me.

"Go back to sleep." His voice is rough, just above a whisper as he has me swooped into his arms, carrying me toward the door.

"What about Zeke?" My voice catches as I glance back at my son, sound asleep in his bed.

Luca carries me out into the hallway and then into his bedroom.

"He's asleep. Zeke will be fine." Luca places me gently on the mattress, and I scoot under the covers.

"I'll be right back." Luca heads out of the bedroom, and there's a soft click of the door down the hall.

My clothes are in Zeke's bedroom on the dresser. So much for changing for bed. Beneath the covers, I slip out of my jeans and toss them to the floor.

Luca steps back into the darkened bedroom and quietly closes the door.

I'm surprised he came to get me, that he even cared enough to check on where I was during the night.

I lay on my side, curled up, facing Luca as he climbs into bed beside me.

"I'm worried about Zeke," I whisper.

"Why?" he asks. He shuffles onto his side, facing me. "He's asleep."

"Did you forget about that little boy, the one your father was holding in the basement?"

Luca winces and frowns, his brow twitching. "Zeke will be fine. You have my word."

"And what if he awakens and goes looking for me?" I don't like worrying that my son might wander through the house alone.

But that's not my only fear.

Any one of Dante's men, or the mafia boss himself, could go into Zeke's room and hurt him.

The dread fills my lungs like poison, making it impossible to breathe.

I struggle to catch my breath, gasping as though I'm drowning and in desperate need of air.

Luca's hand grazes my arm and then rests firmly against bare skin. His touch is simple yet effective, helping me breathe, but his words cut much deeper.

"You're panicking over nothing. Our marriage will keep you and him safe."

I scoot closer, wanting to hold him, embrace him, feel something other than emptiness and fear that are filling the void between us.

"Stick to your side." His brow pinches and he rolls onto his back, determined to keep distance between us. There's frustration in his words, in his face, as he pulls away from me, and I feel chilled.

Any sense of comfort is quickly erased.

"Go to sleep, Harper. It's going to be a long day tomorrow. We don't want to disappoint Dante."

I've already disappointed his parents. I doubt they will ever like me, but I suppose if they accept me and don't cause harm to Zeke, myself, or my loved ones, I can live with that. I don't want to be here, but it's not like I have much of a choice. When the Riccis give an order, you obey.

Saturday morning, I'm shuffled upstairs with Nikki.

Zeke is secured to my hip, although he squirms and wants to be set down.

I ignore his little protests and tickle him, trying to change his mood.

It doesn't help. He makes me think of how perhaps a little Luca may have once behaved, not getting his way and fussing the entire time.

"Do you want me to hold him?" Nikki holds out her hands, offering to take Zeke from me.

Zeke's eyes widen, and he willingly throws himself at her while I'm struggling to hold on to him.

Whether I want it or not, Zeke has already made up his mind. Nikki will hold him.

"Thanks." I hand him over, and then he plays the same wiggle and squirm game with her.

Eventually, she sets his feet down onto the floor.

The door to the suite is closed, so Zeke isn't going anywhere without either one of us noticing first.

I grab the wedding dress, remove my clothes and slip into the gown.

It feels strange, putting the dress on now that Luca and I are already married.

I suppose I never do anything typical. I had Zeke long before I got married.

"Let me get the zipper." Nikki walks over, and I reach for my long hair, pulling it up and twirling it into a bun, holding it up with my hands.

She slides the zipper up the dress, smiling as I spin around slowly to face her. I drop my hair, letting the waves cascade down my back.

"It looks amazing on you. The pictures are going to come out so great today! I can't wait for us to share them with everyone."

I knew the wedding photographs were less about the actual pictures and more about proving our marriage. I'm just not sure who we're proving it to, the mafia family or someone else?

"I'll have Paige come in and help with your hair." Nikki heads for the door. "She does a great job with updos. Unless you'd prefer to keep it down for pictures?" Her hand rests on the doorknob, and Zeke is right at her heels, ready to tear out of the room the moment she opens the door.

Nikki lifts Zeke into her arms, taking him with her out into the hallway.

Quietly, I follow, watching as she wanders through the maze of rooms on the third floor and knocks on a closed bedroom door.

A moment later, Paige pokes her head out, rubbing at her eyes.

"Did I wake you?"

"It's fine." Paige waves her hand dismissively. She pulls the robe tighter around herself. "What do you need?"

Thirty-five minutes later, my hair and makeup are completed, and I'm getting my Cinderella-esque moment when Luca comes to the door of the room where I've been dressing, carrying a pair of dainty heels.

"You look good." I can't take my gaze off Luca, except to mentally undress him.

Standing there, he's holding the silver heels by the straps. "I brought you shoes." He doesn't even acknowledge my compliment or make any mention of how I'm shaping up with the wedding gown.

However, his throat bobs when he swallows, and his jaw tightens like he's grinding his teeth together for sport.

"You didn't have to." I take the heels from his hands and move to sit at the edge of the mattress.

"I did. Dante insisted I bring them up to you." There's no smile on his face. No sign of happiness in his demeanor, and I can't help but hate that I'm the reason he's miserable.

"Thanks." I put the shoes on and then carefully stand, making sure I don't face-plant.

"The photographer is already downstairs." Luca stays by the open door. He doesn't step foot inside the room, but he also isn't walking away. He seems transfixed, staring at me, but he doesn't seem happy.

"I'm ready." I head toward him, and Nikki is right behind me, holding the train of my wedding gown.

Luca steps out of the way, grabs Zeke as my little terror runs out of the room, and he carries him down the stairs with us.

I'm careful on the stairs, holding the banister as I descend the main staircase, although my attention is on Zeke and Luca several steps ahead of me.

By the time we're in with the photographer, Nikki and Paige help with Zeke while the two of us are shuffled from one pose into another.

Most aren't too terrible. We both manage to force a smile. The most awkward is when we're instructed to stare into each other's gaze.

Luca is shooting daggers at me. There's no loving gaze, no warm embrace.

Everything with Luca is frosty and chilled to the bone.

The photographer grumbles after reviewing the images on his digital camera. “These aren’t working for me. We’ll need to take more.”

“Seriously?” Luca’s frustration is exactly how I’m beginning to feel.

“Your wife is perfect. Absolutely flawless. That pure smile and those magnificent eyes. She is like heaven on a canvas. You, on the other hand—” The photographer sighs and adjusts his camera settings, avoiding finishing his own sentence.

Luca growls as he steps toward the gentleman, his eyes tightening and his fists clenching at his side. “Do you make it a habit of hitting on every woman you photograph or just my wife?”

My mouth goes dry. I glance from the photographer to Luca, and they’re head-to-head, about ready to fight. The photographer is scrawny and no match for my husband.

Nevertheless, Luca’s words shock me.

The fact he's behaving quite so protectively is startling. I can't help but stare at Luca, breathless.

He must be acting.

Because when the photographer said truly nice things, I would have expected him to shut him up and comment on how he doesn't know me like Luca does.

I step forward, resting a hand on Luca's arm, desperate to break the tension before something else breaks. "Sweetheart, why don't we take a five-minute break?"

Luca glares at the photographer. "Are we paying you by the hour?"

"Yes, your father is." He glances at his watch, eyeing the time but not hurrying in the slightest.

"Then we are most certainly not taking a break and giving this jackass another cent." Luca is fuming, and I grab his hand, pulling him closer, trying to calm him down.

Although I'm likely the worst person to settle him down since I have the uncanny ability to cause him to argue, to fight, to hate me.

When I touch his hand, my own body relaxes, his energy warm and comforting, and I step closer, cutting the distance between us.

Instinctively, he leans in toward me when I come to rest my forehead against his.

I hear the snap of another photo but ignore the photographer. I reach up, my hands grazing Luca's cheeks, trying to soften his features, the anger that is built into the tension in his neck and shoulders.

My neck is still sore from last night, falling asleep against the wall in Zeke's room, but I ignore the pain.

What I can't ignore is the strained look on Luca's face.

I crack a wry grin and drag my hands down to his hips. "Kiss me," I whisper, hoping that maybe I can get the tension to melt away for both of us.

"What?" Luca stares at me like I've lost my mind.

"Your wife asked you to kiss her." The photographer doesn't have the slightest clue that we're unhappily married. He snaps another picture, but I can only imagine Luca looks constipated or fed up with me.

Either way, the photographs aren't going to be usable.

A sigh slips past Luca's lips, and then I feel his breath mingle with mine, hovering but waiting.

I drag my fingers through his hair, and his eyes close. There's a deep sadness, and it helps not to feel it staring back at me.

I lean in, kissing him, needing a taste, hoping that he'll play along instead of push me away.

The kiss is tentative at first, soft, curious.

His body melts against mine, the icy exterior crumbling away as he pulls me tighter, closer, kissing me deeply.

I hear the snap, snap, snap of the camera.

Luca breaks the kiss and glares at the photographer. "We're not giving you a free show," he growls.

A faint smile spreads across my lips. Even if Luca is pretending to be in love with me, I'll take it. His words make my tummy flutter and my body tingle.

Luca's thumb grazes my bottom lip, his gaze on my mouth.

My heart quickens, and my senses are overwhelmed. Does he want to kiss me again?

How easily it would be to lose myself in him.

I've missed kissing him, touching him, falling into bed with him.

The photographer glances through his camera roll, pausing and zooming in. "I think a few of these will do. Unless you want another few shots? We can call it if you're both satisfied."

Luca untangles from my embrace and stalks over. "Let me see the photos."

The photographer flips through the photos on the digital screen, and Luca's jaw is tight. The latter images must be better than the first ones that we took.

Even Luca seems to relax as he reviews them and sees they're not all bad.

"We're done." Luca turns and heads out of the room. It seems he's leaving me behind until he turns at the door and glances over his shoulder. "Are you coming?" He's short and still a bit testy.

Jealous?

Is that what's seeping out after the compliment the photographer gave me?

"Of course." I smile and follow after Luca.

Just outside the room, Paige and Nikki are entertaining Zeke, rolling a ball back and forth with him, which seems to be holding his interest.

That is until he sets his sights on me. "Mama!" Zeke leaves the ball behind and hurries over, stumbling as he throws himself at me, tripping over the hemline of the gown and the train, which has curled up under my feet without anyone's help walking around.

I bend down, lifting Zeke into my arms. "Were you good for Mama?" I ask, hoping Nikki and Paige would be honest with me.

"He's always a delight." Nikki stands and rubs at Zeke's back as I hold him. "Makes me miss when Luca was that little."

Zeke buries his hands in my chest and then his face, closing his eyes.

Paige stands from the floor with a yawn and stretches. "I think someone is ready for a nap—

Zeke." She's quick to clarify when her yawn reminds me that I'm exhausted too.

"Did you sleep all right?" Nikki glances from Zeke to me.

"He slept great." I don't need to lie to her or explain that I was too afraid to fall asleep here again.

Luca puts an arm around my shoulders. "I slept great too." The smile on his face almost seems genuine, but I can't help but feel betrayed.

He's lying to his mother and to Paige.

"You put me right to bed." He pulls me in for a kiss in front of them, and I can't help but lean into it, knowing that it's not real but not caring.

My brain is screaming at me, knowing he hates me, but his tongue glides past my lips and my body heats up from his touch.

Nikki clears her throat. "Maybe we should give you two some privacy." She takes Zeke with her as she and Paige head down the hallway.

Once we're out of earshot, I raise an inquisitive eyebrow at him. "I put you to bed?" I glare at him. "I can't believe you suggested to your mom that we did *that* under her roof!"

Embarrassment floods through me, making my cheeks burn.

"Wouldn't be the first time." Luca stares at me, and his fingers graze my cheek.

This thing between us, the heat that sizzles, it isn't real.

I just can't fathom why he's pretending.

"What are you doing, Luca?" I know his feelings diminished, or maybe he doesn't like me at all anymore.

It's just the two of us. There's no audience. No show that needs to be put on. Besides, Nikki and Paige can't honestly believe it's paradise between us.

I tilt my head, glancing up at Luca. I want to call him out, argue with him, scream and tell him that he can fool his mom, but he can't fool me.

And that's when I see it. He lifts my chin to his stare. "Kissing you, it just—" His breath is raspy, and he leans in again. "I can't stop myself after one taste. I crave your touch, your taste, the sweet smell of your skin."

His words send tingles through my body. His fingers unclasp the clip in my hair, bringing the curls down around my shoulders in waves.

He grabs a fistful of my hair, tilting my head up, holding me, keeping me under his command. "Tell me to stop, that you don't want this."

But I do want this; I want him, more than I've ever wanted anything. "Never."

He groans, fighting desire but failing as his lips conquer mine, and I relax under his touch, my mouth opening as he deepens the kiss.

I've missed him, missed this, the sweet stolen moments, the simple touch of his hand on my cheek sliding to the back of my neck as he deepens the kiss.

He guides me back against the wall, his lips moving across my collarbone, sucking and nipping at the skin. He sets my body ablaze.

"Dada!" Zeke squeals from around the corner as he comes running in to find us.

Luca freezes, his body grows rigid, and he breaks the kiss. It's like the mood just disappeared from a simple word. Or it could be my son storming in that made Luca uncomfortable.

"Sorry!" Paige chases after Zeke. "Didn't mean to interrupt the two of you. Nikki disappeared into the bathroom, and Zeke wouldn't hold still for two minutes."

Sounds exactly like my son. Exhaling, I force a smile. "It's okay." I reach for Zeke, picking him up and flipping him around in my arms, giving him butterfly kisses over his nose and cheeks.

He squeals and throws his arms at Luca. "Dada!" he chants again, and this time Luca takes him with an awkward smile.

"Are you sure you know what that means?" Luca rubs his nose against Zeke's, and I swear I fall more in love with the two of them every day.

Heavy footsteps tap over the flooring, and I glance in the direction. It doesn't sound like Nikki.

"Are we done here?" Moreno doesn't offer a smile, no hint of warmth. "Your father wants me to take

Harper and Zeke back to campus when the photographer is done."

"I'll need to get changed." I gesture to the dress that I'm wearing.

"Of course." Moreno nods. There's no smile. No kind words. Not even a polite chitchat about the photographer and the pictures we were required to take. "I'll be waiting by the foyer in ten."

He doesn't give me much time.

"I'll watch Zeke while you get changed." Luca continues to cuddle Zeke, but the minute I start to exit into the hallway for the stairs, Zeke starts fussing.

There are no tears yet, but they're inevitable.

"Mama!" Zeke squeals and shrieks.

It breaks my heart. On some mornings when I drop him off at daycare, I experience the same sounds, and it rips me apart inside.

Mondays are always the worst, after Zeke and I spend all weekend together. "It's okay. I can take him." I hold out my arms, and Zeke climbs onto me like a monkey but refuses to let go. “Can you show me which room it is again?”

Zeke’s cheeks are red, his eyes glassy, and he exhales a heavy sigh once he’s in my embrace. He rests his head on my shoulder, and his eyes close. He could use a nap. Makes two of us.

“Of course.” Luca walks alongside me until we reach the stairwell. “Let me take Zeke.”

“Are you sure you don’t mind?” Managing heels and the train of the wedding gown is difficult enough, but doing it up two flights of stairs carrying Zeke is not wise.

Luca must realize the dilemma too. “I don’t want anything to happen to Zeke or to you. We’ll be fine,” he assures me. “You, in those fancy heels and dress, need to be careful.”

“Okay.” I hand off Zeke again, and this time he’s not fussing since the little one has his sights on me the entire time.

Luca leads me to the third floor and to the suite where I had gotten dressed in the wedding gown earlier in the morning.

He opens the suite door, and I step inside. "Can you come in and help me with the zipper?"

Wordlessly, Luca steps into the room behind me with Zeke and secures the door. "Turn around." He gestures with his finger.

I hear the soft plop of little feet as he puts Zeke down onto the floor.

Luca's hands caress my hair, pushing it to one side over my shoulder before he gradually lowers the zipper on my wedding dress.

I let the gown fall to the ground and step out of it, breathing a sigh of relief. I lift the material and place it back onto the hanger.

"Mama!" Zeke squeals and comes running at me, tackling my legs.

Luca covers Zeke's eyes. "Don't look, buddy."

I laugh, shaking my head while I grab my clothes from earlier in the morning. "Why not?"

"He shouldn't see his mother naked."

I glance down at my undergarments. "This is

naked?" I tilt my head to the side. "You and I have a different definition."

I pull my sweater on over my head and reach for my jeans. "And you don't see me covering your eyes."

Luca grins. "Oh, come on, we're past all that."

My gaze tightens. "Are we?" I ask, stepping closer, into his personal space. "Last I checked, we weren't sleeping together. Which means you have no business seeing me naked."

His smile fades, but he doesn't flinch or even glance away. He's staring right through me, and it sends a shiver down my spine. "We're married."

"By contract only." It's the reason I was standing in my wedding gown just minutes earlier, we're both abiding by a legally binding agreement.

Luca leans in, his breath teasing me, making me want to kiss him. His gaze moves to my lips, but he doesn't close the distance. He just hovers and waits, dragging the unbearable tension out, tormenting me. "It's still a very real marriage."

I snort. "You're right, it is. Married and not having sex. Sleeping in separate rooms. Sounds just like a typical marriage." I take a step back, my heart nearly pounding out of my chest.

He grumbles and grabs me by the hip, pulling me closer. "You know that isn't what I meant."

"Do I?" I tilt my head, staring up at him.

"I don't want *that* kind of marriage with you."

"What do you want, Luca?" I ask, my breath catching in my throat.

TEN

DANTE

I slam the door shut, run a hand through my hair and pin my wife with a stare. I'd like to pin her with something else against the door, but she's fuming, and that rage that's focused on me is fucking hot.

Space isn't a bad idea right about now, or else I'll ravish her, and she might bite off my head—something no man ever wants to experience.

"I can't believe you!" Nikki scowls at me, coming head-to-head, although she's technically quite a bit shorter than I am. She stares up at me, her eyes wild, and I swear there's steam emanating off her body.

The heat makes my pulse quicken, as does the desire in her eyes.

Her anger always betrays her body, making her lust for me.

I know every inch of Nikki. I've had every taste of flesh, inch by inch.

She's mine.

Even her anger is mine.

We're not so different.

Nikki was brought up by a father who ran an opposing mafia organization. He's dead now. Can't say I'm sad of that fact. He was a monster who sold his own daughter to me.

"Quit staring at me like that." Nikki smacks my chest with her hand and pushes me backward. "You look like you want to pounce on me. You should be mad too!"

I take a calming breath. Not that it does much. "Mad about what?" I tilt my head slightly, staring at her with incredulous eyes.

Of course, I'm angry, reeling inside.

Luca and Harper are clearly at odds with each other. Throwing them together to wed so quickly may not have been the best idea.

Nikki wanted a swift wedding.

I just wanted Luca working for me.

A wedding was an added little bonus, because Harper is clearly fertile, and I'd like to see my son with an heir before I die.

"He despises her!" Nikki pulls away from me, pacing the length of my office. "I thought a February wedding would cut through the heartache and make them realize they still have feelings for each other."

"It's been a week, kitten."

Nikki's gaze tightens when I use the nickname that I'd given her years ago. Most times, she likes it, but right now isn't one of those moments.

It seems I've angered my little kitten.

"Did they even share a bedroom last night?" Nikki asks.

"He carried her to bed sometime in the middle of the

night. Cameras caught the interaction outside the bedroom."

One of my men informed me this morning of the news.

"That's—something," she whispers and stops pacing. "Maybe there is still hope for them."

"There's always hope. Don't give up. They just need more time to rekindle the romance. I could send them on a honeymoon."

Nikki holds up a hand. "Let's save that for their first-year anniversary gift, when they trust us with Zeke."

"Assuming they make it a year," I grumble. While our family doesn't condone divorce, they could easily live two separate lives. I don't, however, want my son considering that as an option.

"I'm trying. I had the room redone for Zeke and a playroom set up on the main floor." Nikki glares at me. "What have you done?"

"I paid for that damn wedding." I'm still bitter that Harper ran off, leaving my boy humiliated.

Revenge boils in my blood.

Betraying the mafia comes at a cost, a steep price that she'll be forced to pay.

When the time comes, I will make her pay.

Or better yet, my son will take on the cost.

Nikki perches herself at the edge of my desk and scoots back, sitting on the wood, her legs dangling off the side.

Heat builds within me, seeing her on *my desk*.

I stalk toward her, blocking her escape, my legs between hers, spreading her legs farther apart.

A sly smile reaches her face, like she planned this all along.

My *kitten*.

She grabs my tie and yanks me lower, her lips teasing me but not kissing me, yet.

I'll make her want to kiss me.

Nikki's mouth parts, and she stares up at me with a heated gaze, one hand on my tie, the other on my cheek as she grazes my stubble. "I want you to fuck me like you used to, when you hated me."

I can't help but smile. "I never hated you, not even for a moment."

"Even when I was pregnant and trying to escape?" she asks. Leaning back on the desk, her movements drag me closer against her.

My hands firmly plant against the wooden grain, pinning her down.

"Those were the moments I loved you a thousand times more, because I knew you wouldn't make it ten feet from me. I'd never let you run. And if you did escape, I'd have hunted you down, brought you and our baby home."

She kisses me, her tongue wild and her body free. Her arms clawing at me like the kitten she is, her legs wrap around my hips as her mouth is fused on mine.

Fuck, her fervor is hot.

She grinds her hips upward against my groin, and I inhale sharply, pulling apart from the kiss.

I want to kiss her, taste her, devour every inch of her. My mouth descends on her neck, dropping heated kisses while gasping for air.

After all these years together, she still knows how to set me on fire.

My fingers work the buttons on her shirt, pushing the material off her shoulders and letting it fall to the floor.

A trail of kisses across her collarbone makes her moan as I move lower. I unclasp her bra, kissing her shoulders as the straps glide down and the material tumbles to the floor.

She sighs ever so softly, and my lips move back to her chest, one hand cupping and teasing her breast, the other gently teasing her waistband as my fingers deftly move toward the button.

"You always do this," she mumbles. Her fingers tangle in my hair, and I pause with my lips just over a nipple.

"Do you want me to stop?"

She groans and shakes her head no. "I'm going to need confirmation, kitten." I always like hearing her talk during sex. Every word and sensual sound revs me up inside.

"If you stop, I'll kill you myself." There's a slight growl in her voice, and I swear my heart quickens.

"I didn't know anyone else was in the room to murder me." I chuckle, and she snarls at me.

"Kitten, you keep doing that and I'm going to make this *really fucking quick.*"

My cock twitches.

She undeniably has me wrapped around her finger. Not that I'd ever admit such a thing. It would make me look weak.

"Quick isn't bad, as long as you're inside of me." She pushes me back slightly and moves her hands to her pants. She unclasps the button and then wriggles her hips, freeing herself of her pants and her panties in one swift motion.

I undo my belt buckle and work my pants free, letting them hit the floor.

"Did you lock the office door?" Nikki asks, glancing past me.

I don't fucking remember.

"Yes."

I'm not about to stop what I'm doing right now to check. And my men know better than to barge in unannounced. Especially when I'm fucking my wife.

Her screams will be indicator enough to back the fuck off and keep out.

My fingers tease her entrance. Already, she's slick, her legs spread wide for me, and she's a heavenly sight.

I glide two fingers in, her wetness coating me as she gyrates her hips and lets her head fall back. Her back arches, and she clenches onto my fingers.

"Are you trying to come without me?" I stare at her, and a wicked smirk crosses her features as I curl my fingers the way she absolutely adores.

"You feel so fucking good when you do that." Her breath catches in her throat, and her breathing quickens.

I lean down, licking her pussy juices as I withdraw my fingers and she whimpers in protest.

"I want your cock in me."

Her words are like honey to a bear, and I'm ready to pounce and take what's rightfully mine. "Say it."

"Fuck me. I need you to fuck me," she whispers through heavy-lidded eyes.

"Beg me."

"Fuck, Dante." Nikki is at the precipice and I'm the one making her teeter on the edge.

"That's not begging, kitten."

Her voice comes out desperate, and her fingernails claw at my chest, reaching for my cock. "Please, fuck me."

A smirk reaches my lips as I stroke my cock, teasing her entrance, letting her slick juices coat my head. I smack her with the head against her pussy a few times and her hips buck.

"You're going to fucking kill me if you make me wait any longer." She's impatient, and I dare admit I like her neediness when it comes to craving me.

"I would never want to harm you," I rasp and slowly glide my cock into her warmth.

She spreads her legs wider, her back arching as I fill her body and she wraps her legs around me, taking every inch of me, pulling me tighter and deeper.

"Fucking about time," she mutters and smacks my ass.

I chuckle and glide one arm beneath her at her back, and the other stays tangled in her hair, taking a fistful as I carry all the control.

I tug gently, just enough to let her know I'm in charge, and she whimpers and moans.

Her sounds drive me absolutely wild.

Each gasp of breath turns me on even further.

Her cheeks flame, and her body claws at me. Fingernails scraping my ass, climbing up my back, pulling me against her as I try to take command.

Fuck.

Her hips move against mine, and the feeling is absolutely glorious as her insides tighten around my cock, twitching and spasming.

"Don't you dare fucking come yet," I growl.

Nikki whimpers, and the pulsating ceases momentarily as she raises up and bites my neck, leaving a mark on my skin.

"Fuck."

In all the years we've been together, she's never purposely bitten me.

The feeling makes me thrust harder, faster, crave even more of her if that's possible.

I'm inside of her, and I still want more.

I have her heart, her body, and yet the craving overpowers me.

My hands find hers, pinning her down against the desk, my mouth covering hers, pushing my tongue inside, past her lips.

Her hips keep a steady tempo, thrusting up into me, and mine keep the pace, fucking her wildly, with abandon.

The moan rips through her body, coursing at lightning speed as her pussy spasms around my cock.

It is the most amazing feeling, and this time I don't stop her.

"Come for me, kitten," I rasp into her ear before covering her mouth with mine again.

Her tongue is searching for mine, her fingers clenching my hand as I keep her pressed firmly against the wooden desk, and her body curls around me.

The feel of her insides spasming and her moans send me reeling.

I'm right there with her, thrown over the abyss, falling into oblivion, moaning and chanting her name as the heat overwhelms me and I finally let go.

Gasping for air, my heart pounding against my chest, I slowly loosen my grip on her hands and move off her.

Nikki slowly begins to sit up, but I guide her back down. "No, kitten. Lie just like that." I grab her shirt and offer it as a pillow for her head.

I spread her legs, smiling at the sight of my seed dripping out of her pussy.

She laughs and glares at me. "We're not having another baby," she playfully huffs and sits up, shoving me aside.

I've contemplated fucking with her birth control

pills, throwing them down the toilet to ensure I put a baby in her, but she's right.

Now isn't the time. I'm enjoying the fact that I get Nikki to myself.

Selfish?

Probably, but I love not sharing her with anyone else.

"About our first baby—"

"Luca isn't a baby anymore. He's not even a child," Nikki says, correcting me.

I roll my eyes at her. "Obviously, kitten, or he wouldn't be working for me. Speaking of which, I know how to make him more invested in the job."

She exhales heavily through her nose, her eyes tightening. "Whatever you're planning, I hope you know what you're doing."

"I always know what I'm doing," I say smugly.

She smacks my arm and climbs off the desk, redressing. "Just don't let him get hurt."

I grab my pants and get my clothes looking back to normal, reasonably enough.

"Yes, that's my plan, hurt my son," I mock, and she grabs my arm, her little hand pinching the hell out of my muscle. I pretend it doesn't hurt, but fuck, she's got a strong grip on me.

"I will end you if you so much as hurt a hair on his head."

Nikki's always been tough, probably because Gino raised her himself.

"Relax, kitten. Luca isn't a baby anymore. You said it yourself. He can handle the job."

She sighs heavily and releases her grip on my arm. "Don't go screwing this up with him."

"I wouldn't dream of it." My words are a complete truth. There's no reason to lie to my wife.

I have no intention of harming Luca; I want him invested in my business. I want him begging to take over the mafia when I'm too old or dead to carry out orders myself.

I just need him to want it, and right now, I know it's the farthest thought on his mind.

ELEVEN

NOVA

Stretching out on the sofa, I shove my legs over Ashton, and his fingers immediately rub my thighs.

I swear we're trying to watch a movie, but I haven't spent two seconds on the actual plot. Plot, what plot?

Ashton always manages to steal every second of my attention.

"Can you pass me the pillow?" I gesture at the opposite end of the couch to the decorative pillow propped on the side.

Ashton grabs it and teases me with it. "This pillow?"

“Yes.” I hold out my hand, waiting for him to give it to me, but instead, he whacks me with it.

“Pillow fight!” Ashton beams proudly at his assault on me with a pillow.

There’s one pillow at my back, but it’s not quite enough to make me comfortable. I reach for it and get on my knees, trying to gain an advantage as I swat at him with the pillow.

Ashton shifts out of the way, and I leap at him, throwing my body on him with the pillow.

He manages to smack the pillow out of my hands, and it falls behind us onto the floor.

“You jerk!”

Meanwhile, he grabs the pillow he hit me with first and takes another whack at me. It doesn’t hurt other than my pride, which is severely bruised.

I straddle him, vying for the pillow that he lifts above his head, trying to keep out my reach.

He leans forward, which forces me backward, and with my legs at either side, it’s not enough to hold on. I’m forced to wrap my arms around his chest as he bends me backward, the pillow outstretched in his arms.

"Give me a hand!" he shouts, and I glance in the direction of footsteps as Liam emerges from his bedroom.

Liam smirks and shakes his head. "Fat chance I'm getting in the middle of that." He gestures at the two of us. "When are you telling Luca about your situationship?"

Is that what we are?

"Never," Ashton grumbles. "Luca will have my head, and I prefer not to be murdered in my sleep."

I pause and finally let go, the motivation and fun slipping away as I climb back onto my side of the sofa and pretend to watch the movie.

Ashton's brow is furrowed, and he tosses the pillow at me, letting me have it, like I won some grand prize.

Except I feel like everything just turned to shit in a matter of seconds.

Situationship?

Ashton doesn't ever plan to tell Luca about us?

My head is spinning, and my thoughts are reeling out of control.

I can't take it anymore. I stand and toss the pillow at him. "Is that all we are—a situationship?"

Ashton huffs and glares at Liam.

"Why are you looking at him?" I'm waiting for Ashton to answer me.

"Of course not! I like you. We're just ... keeping things quiet. A relationship would mean everyone would know about us."

"Yes, and that's so terrible!" I'm fuming, and I storm to my room. "Don't worry about telling Luca because it's over between us!" I shout over my shoulder before opening my bedroom door and stomping inside. I slam it forcefully behind myself.

Silence fills the void, and tears threaten my vision.

I refuse to cry over some stupid boy who wouldn't even admit to dating me.

Grabbing my phone and Bluetooth headphones, I blast angry metal to dull the heartache.

I will not cry over Ashton Rinaldi.

Flopping onto my bed, I shut my eyes and drown the world out.

Seconds tick away, and my heart pounds with the beat of the music. I don't hear anything, but it's Ashton's hands that jolt me back to reality as he nudges my arm.

My eyes flash open, and I'm ready to kill him. "Go away!"

He gestures to the earbuds, and I remove my earphones, glaring at him.

"I'm not having sex with you ever again. Get out!" I sit up, my feet grazing the floor as I perch myself at the edge of the bed.

His jaw twitches. "You know we're more than a situationship, Nova. I really like you." Ashton shuffles his feet. I can sense he's uncomfortable confessing his feelings after I've screamed at him and broken things off.

Well, good.

He was an asshole.

"Yes, you like me so much that you won't tell anyone about us. Seems like I'm just some girl you like to fuck."

"That isn't true—I mean, I do love fucking you." Ashton quirks a smile.

If I wasn't angry, those dimples and that grin would be turning me on right now. Okay, maybe it is turning me on a little, but I'm still mad at him. I'm just getting flutters in my pussy, and I want it to stop.

"I'm more than just a piece of ass, Ashton. I'm not one of your puck bunnies that you fuck and treat like trash."

His eyes flicker, and there's definitely hurt behind those dark eyes. "I never insinuated that you were. You've always meant more to me than any other girl, Nova."

The way he says my name brings tingles throughout my body.

No, I will not fall weak to his charms. "If this is some grand apology, Ashton, you suck."

He sighs, bends his head forward and closes his eyes. "I am truly sorry. I like you, Nova, a lot." His eyes open, and he stares at me with pure honesty and vulnerability.

My breath catches in my throat, but I don't say anything.

"I shouldn't have let Liam say that about you, about us. You're more than some situationship. I've always wanted it to be more than that with you, with us. You're my girlfriend, and yes, I'm terrified for your brother to find out because he's made it clear he'll kill anyone who touches you."

"You've never had a problem fighting with Luca in the past." I've seen the bloody lip and bruised cheek.

They may be on the same hockey team and best friends, but I've seen evidence of the punches thrown between them.

Two sons, born from different mafia families, they both tend to let their anger lead their hearts. I'm not oblivious to it. My own father is mafia.

But I can't help but hope that Ashton will be different. That, eventually, he'll cut ties to the mafia, and not necessarily his father, but that he'll step out of his footsteps, become his own man.

"I don't want to fight him about this, about us," Ashton says. "I want there still to be an us. I don't want you to walk away from me because of something stupid I said or did. I need you."

I glare at him. "You need me for Psych 101 help."

He doesn't deny it. "I need you for more than just homework and studying, Nova. I want you in my life, as my girlfriend. I enjoy spending time with you, kissing you, and yes, having sex with you. But I love just being around you."

Neither of us has said the L word.

But just him bringing it up, using it to say he enjoys being around me, it makes my heart flutter.

"I'm still mad at you."

Ashton nods slowly. "You can be mad at me, but will you please give me another chance?"

I purse my lips, contemplating what I should do. "Will you tell Luca?" I know it's the one thing he's been avoiding most of all. I'm not too keen on Luca finding out, either, but it seems everyone else already knows. Eventually, word will get out.

"Can you just give it a little more time?" Ashton asks. "I will tell him, I promise. But if he finds out now, during the hockey season, he's going to lose it, and I don't want him screwing up his game."

"You don't want your team to lose." This isn't about Luca, it's about the Narwhals.

Ashton nods. "Yes." He slowly sits at the edge of the mattress, facing me.

"The entire team knows. How long do you think they'll keep our little secret? Even Harper knows. It's not fair to make everyone keep quiet. It's going to come out, eventually."

"Eventually." Ashton stares at me, his hand reaching out, brushing the hair out of my eyes, his thumb grazing my cheek. "Why are you in such a rush to tell him?"

"Are you ashamed of dating me? Is that it?" I can't fathom why he won't tell him, and worrying about Luca getting mad or fighting with him seems like an excuse.

"Of course not. If I were, I'd have broken it off long ago."

"Okay." I'm not sure how to take that comment. I pull

back from his touch, pushing his hand away. “I’m not happy with you right now.”

“I’ve gathered that.” He rests his hands in his lap. “I don’t want us to break up over Luca. It’s ... dumb.”

“My feelings are dumb?” I glare at him.

“That isn’t what I’m saying,” Ashton says and sighs. He rests his hands on his thighs, wiping the sweat that seems to be forming.

Am I making him nervous?

“Then spell it out for me, because I feel like you’re avoiding telling Luca about me, and I don’t know why it worries you so much. Is it because of my father?”

His gaze tightens and then relaxes as he forces a smile. There’s something there, but I don’t push for more answers.

“Luca has a mean right hook, okay?” Ashton laughs and hangs his head. “I don’t want to be out for the rest of the hockey season because he kicked my ass.”

“You wouldn’t fight back?”

"I don't want to, but I might not have a choice, and I know the game is important to him. It's more important to him than it is to me. Hockey is just an outlet for me, a way to face my demons, a place to let them out on the ice. I love playing hockey, but I don't have the same charisma on the ice. I'm not out there trying to go professional."

I quietly listen, reaching for his arm, letting him talk, giving him the chance to explain everything to me.

"If I fight back, and I know I'll end up being forced to do that if we get into a fight, I don't want to ruin his chances this season or next. He could seriously get hurt, because I'm not going to sit there and take a beating because he's angry with me. I'd let him get one, maybe two punches in—he's got a mean right hook, but any more and I can't just let my ass get beaten. I do have a reputation to uphold."

Exhaling heavily, I let my hand find his.

"Thank you for telling me all of that."

"Do you still hate me?" He glances up at me, waiting for my answer.

"I could never hate you."

He brings my hand to his lips, placing a warm kiss on my skin.

"Come here." I scoot closer, my hands against his chest as I raise up, taking a taste from his lips.

He pulls me into his lap, his strong arms warm and comforting after the fight. His fingers dance over my skin, along my hips, up and down my arms. It's like he's memorizing every detail of me.

"I'm sorry," Ashton whispers between kisses. "What can I do to make it up to you?"

I know that telling Luca will just pull us apart again. After the hockey season, which feels like forever, but it's just a few short weeks. The regular season ended at the end of February. The Narwhals are in the NCHC Quarterfinals.

I can't let them risk losing because Luca doesn't have his head in the game. He's their best player, not that I'd tell Ashton. Although I'm sure he already knows, it's why he doesn't want Luca to find out.

It's just a few more weeks; worst case is April if they actually make the National Championship. The Narwhals have never even made the Frozen Four

Semifinals, but they never had Luca and Ashton playing, either.

“Anything you wish.” Ashton drops soft, featherlight kisses across my cheeks and lips. “Your wish is my command.”

A faint smile reaches my face. “Are you a genie now?”

“I could be,” Ashton says. “If I could grant you three wishes, I totally would. What would they be? And don’t give me boring stuff like world peace.”

“World peace isn’t boring!” I elbow him in the ribs.

“Oww!” he whines and then grabs my arms, keeping me from attacking him a second time. “Three wishes.”

“First, would be to let my arms go.”

“Boring.” Ashton rolls his eyes but grins. “Wish granted.” He releases his hold on me.

I laugh. “I’m saving my second and third wish for later.”

“It doesn’t work that way,” Ashton mumbles, and his

hands tease my hips, playing with the waistband of my jeans.

He knows exactly what he's doing, stirring desire within me as I'm situated on his lap.

Damn, he's good.

My cheeks heat up, and my body succumbs to the warmth, relaxing against him.

"Not a wish, but I want you to go tell Liam you're dating me. We're in a relationship. And then proclaim to him how much you care about me."

Ashton's face scrunches. "Do I have to?"

"If you want me to forgive you, yes."

Ashton sighs and rests his hands on my hips. He gently guides me back to my seat on the mattress. He stands, and I do the same, wanting to watch.

"Where are you going?" Ashton glances back at me, surprised that I got up from the bed.

"Oh, I'm one hundred percent here for the show." I follow him out of my bedroom, wanting to witness his grand gesture to Liam about dating me.

As we step out into the hallway, I lean into him, so only he can hear me. "Don't screw this up or you'll be dating your hand indefinitely."

"Harsh." He glares playfully at me and then pinches my butt.

My mouth drops, and he chuckles, striding out into the living room where Liam has perched himself on the couch in front of the television.

"Ashton has something he wants to say," I announce to Liam.

Liam reaches for the remote and hits the button on the television, muting the screen. "I'm listening." He raises an eyebrow, clearly amused and delighted to hear whatever Ashton has to say.

"Nova and I are dating. We're in a relationship, so don't be a dick and call it a situationship. I care about her a lot. She's not just some girl I'm sleeping with; she's my best friend and my girlfriend. Don't ever insult her like that again. She deserves better from you."

Liam's eyes widen. "Got it." He holds up his hand. "Sorry, didn't mean to offend you, Nova."

"It's okay."

"It's not," Ashton says protectively. "No one should be referring to our relationship as anything less than what it is. I care about her, and I want everyone to know that."

Liam watches with curiosity. "Even Luca?" He can't help himself, trying to add more drama.

"Stay out of my relationship, Liam. You don't see me butting into your friends with benefits shit with that girl at Great Falls."

Liam bites his bottom lip and glances at the television. "We broke up."

"Shit. I'm sorry, man." Ashton keeps hold of my hand as he leads me to the sofa.

A heavy sigh parts from Liam's lips as we sit, Ashton beside him and me on the end of the couch.

I'm still without any pillows. Damn, but I'm also not stretching out. "I'm sorry to hear things didn't work out with you and Iris."

He laughs under his breath. "I actually broke it off with her."

"Oh?" Ashton and I both wait for Liam to elaborate, but he doesn't.

Silence fills the air between us.

"What happened?" I finally ask, cutting the tension.

Ashton rests a hand on my thigh, his touch gentle yet firm. It's comforting.

Liam emits a heavy sigh. "You'd laugh and think I'm crazy if I tell you, so can we just ... skip that part and let me just say it's over with Iris?"

"Was it something that happened between you and Iris?" I guess. If it's friends with benefits, maybe someone caught feelings or the sex became something way too kinky for Liam or Iris. That would at least explain his reluctance to elaborate.

"No. It was another girl, whom I'm not even dating. We just kissed." Liam stands, and he's grumbling under his breath, but I can't discern what he's saying.

"You like this other girl." It's an easy guess; why else would he break it off with Iris?

"Yes," Liam says, staring at me. "But I can't like her."

"Why not?" I don't understand the problem.

"It's complicated." Liam walks to the kitchen, leaving Ashton and me on the couch.

I glance at Ashton, and he just shrugs. I stand, following Liam into the kitchen.

"Come on, you know anything you tell us will be kept in the strictest of confidence." I lean against the kitchen cabinets, waiting for Liam to spill the details. I'm a girl for gossip.

"I'm not worried about you telling anyone anything," he says. "It's just, there isn't much to tell. The girl I kissed, I despise. We're complete opposites. She's mean. Spoiled. Rich. The kid is a brat."

"Kid?" I repeat, confused. "I thought it was someone in college. What the hell, Liam? Are you dating someone underage?"

"Fuck, no! She's not a kid anymore. We knew each other as kids, and she tormented me. Hell, I tortured her right back. We have a tumultuous past. And we're not dating. It was one kiss."

"Okay."

Ashton's soft footsteps patter across the floor. He drapes an arm around my shoulders, pulling me close against him. "Is that why you came back to the party last week?"

Liam tenses before nodding. "That's when I ran into the girl and then canceled on Iris."

"Must have been some girl." Ashton whistles and smirks. "You should call her."

"I don't have her phone number, and even if I did, the girl has a mean right hook."

Ashton chuckles. "Liam got beat up by a girl," he sings, teasing his teammate.

"I will deny it and kill you if you tell a soul." A darkness flashes across Liam's features, and Ashton holds his hands up.

"So long as you don't tell Luca about Nova and me, you have a deal."

"I've been keeping your secret, but he's going to find out, eventually."

TWELVE

HARPER

Excitement bubbles in my chest, or maybe it's Zeke who keeps blowing raspberries into me for attention.

Nova, Kensley, and I are seated in the front row. I have Zeke on my lap, and my hands keep repositioning his headphones to block the noise from the crowd.

Zeke doesn't seem to understand he needs to keep the headphones on, and he keeps trying to push them off with his tiny hands.

Bringing a toddler to a hockey game wasn't the best idea, but I want Zeke to see his daddy playing hockey.

Daddy.

Marriage.

It's all still a weird, foreign concept.

It's nearly been two weeks, and while Luca has let me finally climb into bed beside him, nothing has happened. Since the pictures at his parents' house, we've shared a bed, but he's been adamant about putting a vast array of pillows between us, like he's worried he might accidentally roll over and spoon me.

Oh, the horror.

I'm trying my best to give him as much time and space that he needs.

At least I'm not in the room with Zeke anymore, which has landed Zeke sneaking into our room on most nights. I manage to get him back to sleep and tuck him back into his big-boy bed.

But it's been interrupting my sleep.

Luca hasn't budged an inch when Zeke comes barreling into the bedroom in the middle of the night. He's either a heavy sleeper or pretending not to notice. I don't blame him. Zeke is *my* son.

"Look, there's your daddy!" Nova points at Luca on the ice and then tickles Zeke to gain his attention.

Zeke watches with wide, curious eyes as the guys practice before the start of the first period.

"Dada." Zeke points at Luca.

"That's right!" Nova squeals.

She seems a bit more excited than I am, probably because I've heard Zeke refer to Luca as Dada more than once.

"Dada!" Zeke points at Ashton.

"Dada!" Zeke points at Liam.

Well, at least he's recognizing the teammates who live with us.

"Not quite," Nova says and sighs. "Luca is your daddy. Ashton is mine."

My eyes widen, and I smack Nova on the shoulder. "Ashton is not your—oh my God. Can we just not?" I shake my head, wanting to dispel all images of Ashton and Nova that I had previously walked in on and witnessed between the sheets. Although, quite honestly, there weren't many bedsheets covering anything.

Kensley giggles and shoots a look at Nova. "You two did hook up that night! I saw you making out with him at the party."

Nova's face reddens. "Quiet! Luca doesn't know."

"He can't hear us." Kensley gestures between the guys and us. "Relax, I'm not going to say anything. But why can't Luca know?"

Nova blows a strand of hair out of her eyes. "Luca's got big-brother energy. He will beat the pulp out of anyone I'm dating."

"Why?" Kensley asks.

I grin. "Because he can."

Nova and Kensley both laugh, which makes Zeke giggle. It's the most adorable sound in the world. I kiss Zeke's cheeks. "In all seriousness, Luca is going to find out."

"I know." Nova sighs heavily and folds her arms across her chest. She leans back, stretching her legs and then crossing them. "Ashton and I got into a fight about it a couple of nights ago."

"Oh?" I can't help but feel surprised that they're fighting. There hadn't been any sign of it while I've been home. No tension. No spats. If anything, they've been cuddling on the couch watching movies together at night.

It's kind of crazy how Luca hasn't noticed the cuddling, but he just sees Nova as his little sister and Ashton as his best friend. To him, they're just two of his favorite people hanging out together.

"We worked things out. You weren't home when it all went down." Nova waves her hand through the air and then her gaze locks on Ashton. A wry grin crosses her features as she watches him on the ice. "Liam was being a dick and, well, the whole relationship nearly went up in flames. It's better now. I just wish Ashton would find the courage to tell Luca. Not wait until the season is over."

"It could be worse," Kensley says, pointing at Zeke. "This little guy could spill all your secrets."

"Give it another month or two and he just might," I say. Zeke is already babbling a lot more, and while not all of it is decipherable, he is starting to learn to repeat words.

Nova groans. "Just great!"

Ashton skates over to the plexiglass, waving at Nova. "Hey, babe."

"Dada!" Zeke points at Ashton.

Ashton glances over his shoulder, eyes wide, his face turning ghastly as he searches for Luca, who is still in the center of the ice warming up. "Kid nearly gave me a heart attack. Thought someone might be sneaking up on me." Ashton is a bit breathless.

"Break a leg!" Kensley shouts at him.

Nova pales in her seat. "That's for theater! Don't shout that in here unless it's at the other team."

"Sorry! Sorry!" Kensley holds her arms up. "Just trying to cheer you guys on."

"A little too enthusiastically." Nova glares at Kensley, and I swear I see a bit of jealousy burn right through her.

Ashton glances over his shoulder once more, and when he realizes Luca isn't watching, he blows Nova a kiss. "See you after the game, babe. Are you coming tonight to the after-party?"

"Wouldn't miss it for the world," Nova says.

Nova and Ashton are quite adorable together. While I know Luca won't be happy with the news, maybe I can help smooth things over after they tell him they're dating. It's not like Nova is in high school anymore. She's eighteen, an adult, and in college.

At least she's making good choices. Ashton isn't a bad option in terms of boyfriends, although I'm not sure I'd have thought that a few months ago.

Ashton points at Zeke. "Love the look," he says, giving a wave at my son.

Zeke's swimming in the child-sized jersey we managed to snatch up this afternoon. It's over his winter clothes, and he's still swimming in it.

"Catch you later." Ashton skates backward, showing off as he heads back toward Luca, who is practicing shooting goals.

The team then returns to the locker room before entering the ice arena again, this time for the game.

I can't help but feel butterflies in my stomach. I want Luca to do well, to win. Is this how he feels before every game? I also don't dare admit to anyone that

I'm disappointed Luca didn't come over and say hi to Zeke or to me during practice. But we came here to support him, not make it about us.

The game ends with a final score of 1-3. The Narwhals win, and Luca is flying high, given that he scored two of the three goals tonight.

He skates over to us after the game, and my heart quickens, surprised he noticed us. He barely paid us any attention tonight, but maybe that's what he needed to win.

"Hey." Luca waves at Zeke, who just stares at him.

Kensley and Nova head out together, leaving me standing alone with Zeke. I don't mind it. They're both getting ready to head to the party. I'm getting ready to take Zeke home to bed.

"It's past his bedtime," I explain when Zeke cuddles into my arms and his eyes flutter closed.

"Go, take him home. Don't wait for me tonight."

"Have fun at the party." I don't even ask if he's going. I'm assuming that he is. The rest of the team is going to the old place where we used to live. Chase is hosting the party along with his new roommates, who also play for the Narwhals.

“Thanks,” he says, and his smile is genuine. His eyes flicker for a moment. “Are you okay with me going?”

“Just don’t hook up with any puck bunnies, but I’m happy you’re going out with the guys.” I am glad he has friends and he can still go do things with them. Just because we’re married and I have Zeke, doesn’t mean that he has to give all of it up. I don’t want that for him.

He laughs under his breath. “Don’t worry. I hear my room in the old house isn’t vacant any longer.”

That doesn’t make me laugh or smile.

We had good memories in his bedroom. The new house, all I feel is cold and distant in our new room. I can only blame myself for that frigidness.

“Bad joke?” Luca offers a crooked grin, and my stomach dances with those little butterflies.

“I miss those days,” I say, wishing the plexiglass wasn’t the only thing standing between us.

Luca nods. "Me too." He takes off his helmet and rubs at his hair. "I should go shower up. See you later tonight?"

"Pillows and all," I mutter under my breath.

His gaze tightens, but he nods. I'm not sure if he caught what I said or not. The crowd has dispersed, so it's not nearly as loud as it had been earlier.

"Give Zeke a goodnight kiss from me," Luca says.

I pause, surprised. He's never tucked Zeke into bed. I'm not sure I've ever seen him give my son a kiss or say that he loves him.

"Yeah, will do." I force a smile but can't help but feel confused.

Luca glances around me. "Do you have a ride home? Where'd Kensley and Nova go?"

"They're heading to the party. I walked here with Zeke. I'll walk back. It's fine, there's plenty of people out tonight, and the weather is nice."

"It's single digits outside. It's not nice. Just wait by the locker room. I'll drive you back to the house before the party."

"You don't have to do that, Luca."

"I'm not asking. Wait for me outside the locker room."

I give a curt nod. "Yeah, sure."

He skates off to shower and change. I wander through the stands, making my way toward the entrance of the Narwhals' locker room.

A few other girls are standing around waiting, Nova and Kensley included.

"Hey!" Nova's eyes widen, surprised to see me and Zeke. "I thought you were taking the little tiger home for bed?"

"We are, but Luca is driving us home. He didn't want me to walk alone."

Kensley smiles and leans against the wall. "That's really sweet of him."

Nearly thirty minutes later, Luca steps out of the locker room, Chase and Ashton right behind him.

Luca's hair is wet, and a few water beads drip down his neck as he wipes them with the back of his hand. "I'm going to drive Harper and Zeke back home, then I'll be at the party. Nova and Kensley, Chase is going to drive you to the party. I'll take you guys and Ashton home after."

"Here, let me take him." Luca offers his arms out to hold Zeke.

"Are you sure?" Zeke is nearly asleep. His eyelids keep fluttering open and shut as he fights it.

"You've been holding him all night. Let me give you a break for a few minutes."

I manage to untangle Zeke from my grip and hand him over to Luca. "Thanks."

Zeke's eyes widen as he changes from me to Luca, but then he settles right back down and shuts his eyes, cuddling Luca.

Within seconds, my little toddler is snoring soundly, which is going to be problematic because I have to put his winter coat and hat on him.

"You played well today." I am really proud of Luca, he excels quite well at hockey. Maybe he can make a professional career of it and steer clear of his father's business.

"I did okay," Luca says modestly, offering a wry smile. "It was a good game."

I button my coat and slip on my hat. We approach the door outside but pause while I manage to wrangle Zeke's coat on him.

He fidgets and grumbles, his eyes opening and shutting. He doesn't want to stay awake, and he also doesn't seem to want to put his coat on, but I manage to get it on with Luca's help and then I zip it quickly while he cuddles Zeke, bouncing him in his arms to get him to settle back into slumber.

I pull the hood up over his head since getting a hat on him right now will just be another fight.

I slip my gloves on as we head outside into the chilly night air and hurry across the parking lot to Luca's car.

"Thanks again for driving us."

"Of course. I wasn't about to let my wife walk with our son alone at night."

Wife.

Our son.

Luca doesn't usually refer to Zeke as anything but *my* son. It sounds odd coming from his lips, but I have to admit that I like it.

"How long have you been waiting to call me your wife?" I smile jokingly.

He laughs under his breath. "Just trying it out. It does sound odd, doesn't it?"

"It's new. But I like it." I appreciate that he's trying, and while he may not have forgiven me entirely for running off on our wedding day, perhaps it's time that we can finally move forward together.

"Me too." Luca smiles and unlocks the car door, opening the back seat. He gets Luca situated into the car seat and secures him.

I watch, making sure everything is correct, and he's buckled up tight before I climb into the front seat.

Silence fills the car, but it's a comfortable quietness that I quite enjoy. The car takes a few minutes to heat up, but by the time we get to the house, it's warm and cozy.

"Wait," Luca says before he parks the car and I climb out.

I turn to face him, and he pulls up in the parking space outside the house, the engine running with the heat still on full blast.

He reaches across the seat, his hand grazing my cheek, his fingers in my hair as he leans closer and pulls me toward him. His lips find mine, and while I'm surprised he's kissing me again, my body remembers everything from before and warms instantly to his touch.

There's no fighting desire, nor would I want to with Luca.

My lips part, and he hungrily devours me, tongues dueling as the world around us seems to disappear.

Heat peppers my skin. His lips move across my neck and back to my lips again, fueled with need.

"I've been dying to kiss you." He leans his forehead against mine, breathless.

"Do you want to come inside?" I ask, offering him more than just a kiss for tonight.

His lips crush mine again, and then he unbuckles my seatbelt, his fingers roaming over my body, setting me aflame.

"Yes," he rasps, panting heavily.

He shuts off the car, and he hurriedly unbuckles and carries Zeke up to the front door while I fiddle with the keys. My hands are shaking.

Luca smiles that sweet and warm grin that melts my insides. "You've got it." His thick and raspy voice sends warm tingles throughout my body.

I slide the key into the lock, and it turns, unlocking the door.

"Good girl," he whispers, and I swear I shudder from his voice and words alone.

I help Zeke out of his coat, shoes, and then my own winter clothes before taking him from Luca.

Luca removes his shoes and coat, and a minute later, he's standing in the doorway watching me get Zeke ready for bed.

Usually, he doesn't seem interested. Tonight, he's watching everything. Taking mental notes as I gather his pajamas and change his diaper.

I don't read him a story tonight. It's well past Zeke's bedtime, and I tuck him in, giving him lots of hugs, kisses, and cuddles.

Luca disappears and a minute later comes back sporting a stuffed dragon. “I thought maybe he could sleep with this little guy.”

Zeke reaches out for the dragon and cuddles it tight to his chest, shutting his eyes.

I pull the covers up around him, giving him one more kiss before shutting off the light and closing the bedroom door.

“That was really sweet of you, giving him that dragon.”

“I picked it up at the hotel gift shop last week at our away game.” Luca pulls me against him, his hips finding mine as he pins me against the wall, just outside Zeke’s bedroom door. “I’ve been dying to taste your lips again.”

My eyes close and I raise up, brushing my lips against his, needing him, wanting him, desiring forever with him.

He’s hungry, and his need is insatiable. He pulls me with him backward, toward our bedroom and then lifts me, my legs around his waist as he brings me into our bedroom, pressing me against the door, closing it behind us.

"I want to fuck you, princess."

I don't argue the nickname. Right now, he could call me anything and I'd oblige.

"Are you going to be a good girl for me and do as you're told?"

"Yes," I rasp, eyes shut, reveling in the feelings he stirs within me.

"Good girl."

I moan, my body doing delicious things from just his words alone, and he carries me over to the mattress, laying me down on the plush material.

He releases his grasp of me, and I whimper in protest, missing his warmth. If he's teasing me and decides to leave, as some retribution for the past, I'll end him.

He stands at the edge of the bed, removes his shirt and then his pants.

He's stunning and absolutely gorgeous, with his chiseled abs. His body is clearly that of an athlete, which just makes me feel slightly more insecure about my own self.

Luca leans down, pressing his body into mine, and I can feel his cock poking me. "You're wearing too many clothes, princess. Do I have to do all the work tonight and undress you myself?"

A coy smile crosses my face. "I'd like that."

He laughs. "I bet you would."

"Get undressed and onto all fours."

I quickly disrobe, and he smacks my ass the moment I'm naked. "Hey! What was that for?" I ask, my bottom his for the taking. I'm naked and feeling quite exposed and vulnerable on all fours, as he stands behind me.

"What isn't it for?"

I glance over my shoulder at him, and he's smirking. His hands smooth over my bottom before walloping it again.

"Oww! Quit spanking me." I roll around onto my butt, which stings, but at least I'm seated and he can't whack me again.

"Quit being a spoiled brat." His gaze tightens, and I sit up on my knees.

"The only brat I see tonight is you." I grab a pillow and smack him with it against his chest.

He barely moves, his body practically like iron against the soft material, and he raises an eyebrow. "Are you done bratting?"

"Is that even a word?" I choke out and wallop him again with the pillow.

He grabs it, this time stopping me, but it still manages to land a blow to his chest. However, he's managed to steal the pillow, yanking it from my hands. He tosses it across the room. "Are you looking for a pillow fight? Because I'll have you know I'm the reigning champion."

I snort with laughter. "I bet you are."

I leap for the pillow, but he has other ideas, tackling me against the mattress, pinning me down. "This is far more fun," he says as his hands restrain me while his lips dance over my neck.

I shiver and moan, my body instantly responding. My nipples harden as his chest brushes against mine, and I wrap a leg around his, pulling him closer.

"Fuck," I moan as his mouth does that thing where his tongue teases the sensitive spot on my neck and then he moves to my ear. "You're going to kill me," I groan as my body writhes under him, but he doesn't release his hold on me.

"I think you're exaggerating, princess." His lips move back against my neck, pleased when my hips begin gyrating, desperate for more. My other leg wraps around his and I wrestle us around, using my hips and my weight while he's kissing my neck, to put him on his back.

He laughs and leans into the mattress, a huge smile spread across his face. "Are you planning on dominating me tonight, princess?"

That nickname is beginning to get on my nerves. "I'm. Not. A. Princess," I seethe at him and pretend to bite, but I keep enough distance not to physically nip at him.

Luca's grin doesn't falter in the slightest. He's not afraid of me. Not that he should be, but still, he's having way too much fun thinking he's in control.

Straddling his hips, my hands press his arms into the bed. I glance around, not having anything I can easily tie him up with, which leaves my strength versus his.

I'm well aware that I'm no match, but maybe that works in my favor.

"Of course, my mistake." He's grinning up at me, his gray eyes a lighter hue of silver and blue I've never seen before. It's mesmerizing, just like everything else about him.

For a moment, I lose myself in the way he looks at me. My pulse races, heat curling low in my stomach, and I can't decide if I want to win this game or surrender to it completely.

Surrender to him.

"If you call me princess one more time," I growl at him.

Luca arches an eyebrow, feigning innocence, but there's a glint of challenge in his eyes.

He shifts beneath me, his cock hard and pulsing between us, and his smirk widens. He knows exactly what he's doing to me, and he's enjoying it too.

"What will you do if I do?" he taunts softly, his voice

barely above a whisper against my skin, daring me to act on my threat.

Anyone else, and I'd hate them for it, but I could never hate Luca.

A wicked smile flickers across my lips as I lean closer. "You really want to find out?" I tease, letting my voice drop to a husky whisper.

I hear the soft gasp as I grind my hips against his, and he's fighting temptation.

My fingers tighten around his wrists, daring him to push back, but he stays perfectly still, eyes locked on mine, hungry and unflinching. For a split second, it feels like we're suspended in time, tangled in possibility, each breath charged with anticipation.

"God, I really do," Luca rasps, and his eyes fall shut as I tease him with my hips.

He's treading carefully, trying to hold on as heat flares between us, and I release my hold on his arm long enough to let my fingers trail down to his cock.

I want to touch him, stroke him, make him scream my name and have him forgive me. Each breath he takes is slow and thick. Heat floods between us, just listening to his breathing, my heart thundering as he rolls us quickly around and I'm flat on my back.

"Having fun yet?" He beams down at me.

My fingers tease the head of his cock, and his eyes flutter closed as his head lolls back, enjoying my touch.

I guide my fingers down his shaft and listen to each raspy breath and gasp for air that he craves, thrilled that I'm responsible for those sinfully beautiful noises that he makes.

"Just getting started, princess," I mock.

His eyes scowl at me using that nickname on him. But before he can say anything further, I'm guiding his rock-hard cock inside of me and I've silenced him.

There's a first for everything.

His eyes blissfully shut, and my heart thunders at the feeling as I take all of him deep inside of me.

Luca pulls out, pushing me away forcefully.

"What—"

“Condom,” he mutters and rolls over to the nightstand to grab one.

Shit.

I can’t believe I forgot the condom. But we’re not with any other partners, at least I haven’t been, and I don’t think Luca has been unfaithful to me.

“I’m on birth control,” I say, hoping that will ease his concerns.

“Right.” He tears the foil packet and sheaths the condom on his cock before climbing back onto me. “Now, where were we?”

I smile, letting him lead this dance because, right now, I don’t care who’s top or bottom. We could be fucking standing, and it wouldn’t matter. I just want Luca, *now*.

“You were about to fuck me because I called you *princess*.”

My reminder is all that he needs because he’s back in control, his cock poised at my entrance and then pushing in, inch by inch.

Every thrust is glorious and feels amazing.

He stretches my insides, moving deeper with each stroke, and I wrap my legs around him, wanting to take all of him.

"Fuck," I rasp, my fingernails scraping at the sheets, the bedding, and then at Luca, craving as much contact as possible, and yet it never feels enough.

My breath comes out in ragged gasps, the room heating up with every movement.

Luca's name slips past my lips in a desperate whisper, my body arching toward him, chasing the electric feeling that builds between us.

Already, I'm so close, but I want him there right along with me. My fingernails mark him, claiming Luca as mine as I claw at him, needing more.

He grabs my hands, pushing them into the mattress at my sides, pinning me down.

His body is like molten lava, flooding me with heat, fire, desire, as I chant his name over and over again.

My body arches, toes curling, as I chase the spark, falling into oblivion.

He's right there with me, his lips fused on mine, silencing the last of my moans and pleas as his tongue pushes past my lips, spilling all of himself inside of me.

A moment later, he rolls off me to remove the condom and clean up. He's breathing heavily, my heart hammers against my ribcage as I still attempt to catch my breath.

He lies down with me, pulling me against his chest as he spoons me.

My eyes close, sated.

It's been too long since he's held me. The feeling alone is warm and comforting. I struggle to stay awake. His soft kisses on my shoulder lull me to sleep.

I don't know how long it's been, but I feel the bed shift and hear the sound of Luca getting dressed. "Are you going to the party?" I yawn, pulling the sheets up around myself.

Luca tosses me my jersey that I wore earlier to the game, so that I have something on when Zeke inevitably wakes and tears into our bedroom.

It's been a bad habit since I started sleeping in his bedroom.

I sit up, pulling the jersey over my head. My eyes are heavy. I want to fall back to sleep in Luca's arms, but I don't think that's happening again tonight. At least not until he comes home.

"Just for an hour, maybe two at most. I need to pick up Kensley, drop her at the dorms and then bring Nova, Ashton, and Liam home."

"Can't someone else do it?" I yawn, crawling back under the covers.

"I don't trust the guys will be sober. I'll be back before you know it." Luca strides over and plants a kiss on my forehead.

"Goodnight, princess," I mumble, trying to rile him up.

He growls and captures my lips in a heated kiss, his fingers tangling in my hair as he pulls me tight against him. "Keep calling me that, princess, and you'll find your bottom scorched."

THIRTEEN

LUCA

It takes every ounce of energy to leave the house, the warmth of my bed where Harper sleeps. It's been weeks since I've touched her, caressed her skin, kissed and worshipped her body.

A part of me wants to stay in bed, but I promised the team I'd be there, and I also made a promise to my friends that I'd drive them home tonight.

Besides, it'll just be a few hours at the party and then I can curl up with Harper for the rest of the night. We have the rest of our lives together.

I head up to the old place I was living in last semester.

From the outside, the house looks the same.

The front door is unlocked, and I let myself in, shutting the door behind myself. The inside is warm, toasty, and loud.

Music pumps all around us. Chase really likes to turn the speakers up, and he's definitely redecorated. The place screams bachelor pad, and the smell is a bit stale.

Kensley and Brooks are hanging by the kitchen. He's leaning against the wall; she's got a drink in hand, laughing at whatever he's saying. There's definitely a vibe there, and Brooks is a good guy. He's the least annoying freshman on the team.

It's clear they're flirting. His body language screams that he's interested; leaning in, he brushes the hair away from her eyes and keeps his hand on her cheek for a moment.

I look away; it's not my business what Harper's best friend does or who she's into.

The sofa in the living room is occupied by Chase and a girl I don't recognize. They're both bonding very intimately.

Ashton and Nova are seated across from them on the loveseat, which I'm not thrilled with the name, but it's just a chair. They're chatting up a storm. Nova stands, drink in hand, swaying her hips to the music.

She's clearly had enough to drink.

Thank God, Ashton is watching her tonight.

It's nice not to have to worry about my little sister. I head past Kensley and Brooks into the kitchen, grabbing a plastic cup with punch. No doubt there's a shit ton of liquor mixed in.

While I'd prefer a beer, it looks like this is the drink of choice tonight.

I'll take it.

It's better than hanging out at this party sober without Harper.

I don't plan on having more than one drink. Okay, two max.

My mind flashes back to tonight, seeing Harper at my game with Zeke, both of them wearing Narwhals jerseys. I wanted to skate over before the game started, but I knew she'd be my biggest distraction.

Not necessarily in a bad way, but I needed to concentrate.

I have to make it pro.

It's the only way to escape Dante's arrangement with me working under him.

And while it would only be a temporary fix, if I can make it big enough, he won't want me involved in the business. There'd be too big of a spotlight, a national audience curious about me when I do eventually retire.

Hockey has to be my way out of Breckenridge. Away from the life Dante has chosen for me and for my family.

I take a swig of the electric punch, and boy, does it ever leave a bite. The sting is welcoming as it slides down my throat. I pour another ladle into my cup and then head to the living room to hang out with Ashton and Nova.

I'm surprised Ashton hasn't been bedding any girls recently, but I actually appreciate that he's keeping his bedmates out of the house.

Knowing Ashton, he's likely hooking up with girls in their dorm rooms, which works for me, less drama.

Heading into the living room, Nova is dancing and swaying to the music. She takes another sip from her red plastic cup.

Ashton is clearly talking to her, and by the looks of it, he's probably getting annoyed with her for drinking. The same way my little sister rattles me when she doesn't listen.

Siblings.

Nova climbs onto the wooden coffee table, and I hurry closer, worried she'll fall in those heels, or worse, the table will collapse under her.

I reach out a hand. "Come on, get down, Nova. You've had enough to drink."

Nova giggles, her words slurring. "I have an announcement to make!" she shouts. A few of my teammates who aren't in the middle of a make-out session look her way.

"Nova," my tone scolds, but she waves me away.

"Someday, I'm going to marry Ashton Rinaldi." Her arms stretch out for him, her doe eyes batting wildly.

"We're going home," I growl and grab her hips, putting her over my shoulder.

My little sister is embarrassing herself. She's clearly had too much to drink.

"Put me down!" Nova bangs on my back with her fists. "Ashton, tell him to put me down."

Her words slur and her body wiggles as she fights me.

Ashton stands and strides the couple of feet closer toward me. "You should listen to your sister, and put her down."

My gaze tightens on Ashton.

He's my best friend.

Why is he telling me what to do with my little sister?

"She's drunk. I'm taking her home. We're leaving, now. Go get Kensley and Liam." I turn to head for the front door.

"Put my girlfriend down, now," Ashton says, and for a moment, my world spins.

"Girlfriend? You're dating *my* sister?" Heat floods my face, and my heart thunders in my chest.

I stalk past Ashton, putting Nova down on the sofa. "Stay," I growl, warning her not to move.

Nova doesn't listen.

She never listens.

Standing, she fumbles toward us. "Please don't be mad, Luca." Nova bats those baby-blue eyes at me, but where it might work for Ashton, it does nothing for me.

I ignore Nova and grab Ashton with one hand, yanking him closer to me, our faces mere inches apart.

Heat licks my skin. My blood runs hot like molten lava. "One rule. I only ever had one fucking rule," I seethe between clenched teeth.

My jaw ticks and I shove him backward, my hands clenched into fists at my side.

"Look, I'm not just sleeping with your sister—"

I lunge at Ashton, grabbing him by the lapels of his shirt, throwing him up against the living room wall. "I warned you not to touch my sister!"

"I care about her, Luca. She isn't just some girl I'm sleeping with."

His words hit me harder than any punch to my body could. "I don't believe you! I've seen the girls you take to your bed, a new one every night."

Nova watches, wide-eyed, and Liam comes barreling around the corner, yanking me back from Ashton.

"This isn't a fling, not for me." Ashton's gaze flickers from me to Nova. The air hums with electricity.

Brooks grabs my other arm, Liam on my left, Brooks on my right, keeping me from attacking Ashton. "We've all known," Brooks says, his calmness only making me angrier.

"Everyone?" I seethe, my eyes growing wider as I glance around the room.

I glare at Kensley. "Even you knew?"

Kensley nods faintly. "I saw them making out months ago when you guys were living here."

"This has been going on for months?" Shock doesn't even begin to describe the gut-wrenching feeling of having been lied to, betrayed by my closest friends, and my teammates.

"We weren't sure how to tell you." Ashton stares at me, worry lines etched across his brow.

Nova steps closer to me and nods at Brooks and Liam. They loosen their hold, finally letting my arms free, but they're standing guard in case I go after Ashton again.

"I wanted to tell you," Nova says, reaching out, her hand gently on my arm. "Ashton and I were fighting just this week about when and how to tell you."

"There shouldn't have been anything to tell." I shoot a glare at Ashton. "I warned you—all of you—" I glance around the room at my teammates, "to stay away from my little sister."

"Luca," Nova's voice is soft, calm, she's trying to be reassuring, but it isn't calming the adrenaline surge that pours through me. "I'm not a little kid. I'm in college now. You can't expect me not to date."

I know that, and I never expected her not to date. "You can date whomever you like. Just not one of these guys," I snarl, pointing at Ashton. "Hockey players are the worst—"

"You're one of them!" Nova shouts at me. "Do you see me stopping Harper from dating you?"

“That’s different.”

“How?” Nova glares at me. “We’re both freshmen. We’re both dating hockey players.”

“I’m not a player!” Doesn’t she realize how different Ashton and I are?

Ashton steps closer to Nova, placing an arm around her waist. “I’m not that anymore; your sister changed me.”

I don’t believe Ashton. He swore he’d never fall in love, that love was a notion conceived entirely by the media. He didn’t want a relationship; he only wanted to fuck a new girl every night.

I want to rip his arm right out of the socket and I step forward, Liam holding me back. “Don’t do it.” Liam’s voice is in my ear.

“Why the hell not?”

“For starters, your hockey career,” Liam says. He keeps a firm hold on me. “You assault him, and you’ll be off the team. Your precious career, gone. Your future with the NHL, nonexistent.”

I grind my teeth together and exhale heavily through

my nostrils. I feel like a dragon with steam emanating, waiting to douse Ashton with fire.

Fuck me.

"Stay the hell away from my sister!"

Nova's eyes tighten. "I get it. You're mad. Angry that we lied to you. I'm sorry we didn't tell you when Harper found out. We shouldn't have made her keep our secret, but you have to see this from our point of view—"

Wait.

Harper knew?

Those are the only words I hear, and they ring loudly in my head, like a gunshot going off.

If I wasn't dying inside before, I certainly am now.

She lied to me.

Again.

"I'm done." I shove Liam off me and head for the front door. "I'm going home. If you want a ride, you better get your ass to my car before I leave."

The drive home is thick with tension. I drop Kensley off at her dorm before heading home. Nova is in the front seat, while Liam and Ashton sit in the back.

Thankfully, Ashton and Nova were smart enough not to sit together in the car, or I might have made them both walk home in the brutal chill. Doesn't matter to me that the wind chill is in the negatives outside.

Silence fills the empty space, and as we get home, I storm into the house, heading right for the bedroom.

I slam the door, momentarily forgetting that Zeke is asleep right next door, and grimace when I hear his cries.

"Fuck me," I grind between clenched teeth.

"Luca?" Harper's groggy voice stirs a fire deep within me, and I push it down, silencing the desire.

"You lied to me," I bite, my words as cold as the night air outside.

Harper rubs the sleep from her eyes as she glances at the clock and sits up. "What?" She's groggy and disoriented for a moment. I recognize the confusion, but I don't fucking care.

"You should have told me!"

She collapses back onto the bed. "You're going to have to spell it out for me. I don't know what you're mad about, Luca."

"Ashton and Nova—and you knew." The heat emanates throughout my entire body. As much as I want to kick her out of the bedroom, it is our room. But maybe she should go sleep on the couch or in Zeke's room on the twin mattress.

A heavy sigh spills past her lips, and she pats the bed beside her—the empty space, my space. "Come, let's talk."

Heat burns through my body. I yank my sweatshirt over my head. I should get changed for bed, but there's no sleep in my near future. I'm too pumped with anger, fueled by the fire that Harper created. "I don't feel like talking."

Harper's words are soft, disarming, but they don't calm me. "So, you just feel like yelling?"

I turn my back on her, facing the mirror. It's dark. I can't see her reflection or my own at this hour. I strip out of my clothes, finding a clean pair of boxers and a t-shirt to put on. Sleeping next to her naked is too intimate tonight.

Not that we haven't already done *that,* but it doesn't change the fact that I'm angry with her.

"You lied to me."

Harper sighs and sits up again in bed. Her voice is quieter, and it should relax me, but instead, it irritates me.

"I walked in on Ashton and Harper—doing things." She gestures with her hands and points to the door. "Down the hallway."

"How long?"

She bites her bottom lip and winces, glancing away. "A while."

"How. Long." The tone in my voice grows more perturbed that she isn't answering my question.

"A while. It was before our wedding but after we moved into this house. I don't know the exact date and time."

Is she being snarky with me? I huff loudly enough

for her to hear me. "So, you thought keeping secrets from me was a good idea?"

She opens and closes her mouth, perhaps deciding on how to answer. Her silence fills the void between us. Eventually, she finally answers when I stare at her, waiting for her to tell me the truth. "I shouldn't have agreed. I just ... I didn't feel it was my place to say anything. I told them both that they needed to tell you."

I grumble and snarl at Harper. "Yeah, well, neither decided to do that. Instead, I had to find out at the party, when Nova announced her love for Ashton."

"She what?" Harper's eyes widen.

"She proclaimed she was going to marry him. Ironic, considering Ashton practically did the same thing in that damned house and said he was going to marry you."

Harper rubs at her temples. "Ashton only said that because your father orchestrated the marriage. He wanted you to be free and me to be wed into the family to keep my mouth shut about that poor kid."

"Not the same thing." I pace the length of the bedroom. I can't sit still, and I certainly can't lie down. "Ashton proclaimed his love for you long before you and I even had our first kiss."

"I-I don't even know what to say to that, Luca. I've never had feelings for Ashton." Her brow is pinched, and the longer I stare at her, the more my body reacts, wanting her, craving her touch.

Her voice is soft, sweet, captivating, like a siren's song, luring me to her.

I reject it.

I keep pacing, forcing distance between us because that's the only thing keeping me rational and not giving in to temptation.

"My point is that Ashton doesn't fall in love. This thing with Nova, it's going to blow up, and when it does, we live together. What then?"

Harper climbs out of bed, the jersey loose over her curves but hanging just above her thighs.

She looks strikingly hot and sinful.

I inhale sharply, desperately pushing thoughts of Harper naked from my mind, because I know she's wearing nothing underneath that jersey.

"I'm sorry I kept the truth about Ashton and Nova from you. I wanted them to tell you. I told them they needed to tell you—"

"And when they refused, you should have come to me yourself. You're my wife!"

Harper momentarily closes her eyes for a brief second and exhales through her mouth. She's trying to remain calm. I can sense that I'm rattling her, and I smirk, knowing that I have that power over her.

"I may be your wife, Luca, but you don't love me. You never have. You can't demand that I don't keep secrets from you when you're keeping secrets from me."

She steps closer to me, but I take a step backward, stumbling into the dresser against the wall. I push off it and shift my weight, turning to keep away from her but also not be backed into a corner or wall.

"What secrets have I been keeping? Because I've been brutally honest with you."

Her hand reaches out first, her fingers grazing my arm, and I yank my body away from her reach. "Don't do that."

"Do what?" she asks, her voice soft and sweet. She's anything but innocent.

"Try to coax me into forgiving you. I can't forgive you, Harper. I won't. Not this time." Heat coils around my heart, and I move farther from her reach.

"Instead, you're going to hate me forever? It wasn't my secret to tell, Luca. Are you going to never talk to your wife again?" Her eyes flicker, and it's obvious she's hurting. I hate being the cause of that pain, but she caused mine first.

Maybe it's childish.

Should I forgive her?

She's not the one shacking up with my sister.

"Ashton never should have touched Nova," I growl, redirecting my anger at him. But he's not in the bedroom.

I storm out of the bedroom and head down the hall. If Nova and Ashton are sharing a bed together, I'm going to kill him.

"Luca, wait." Harper hurries to catch up to me, her voice a harsh whisper. As I rush past Zeke's door, I realize why she's keeping her voice down, and I grimace.

I do not want to ruin things for Zeke.

I don't want to wake him.

I don't want to become my father.

I'm overwhelmed.

Burdened.

Each breath comes out heavier as I gasp for breath. I feel the edge of a breakdown coming. I'm teetering on the ravine, and in moments, I'll be free-falling into oblivion.

Her soft touch is on my back.

Harper.

I don't pull away. A small part of me wants to push her away, tell her not to touch me, to leave me be. But I don't move. My legs crumple to the floor, her arms around me, sheltering me.

Each breath of air feels impossible to take.

My lungs struggle and burn as I gasp and clutch at the air with my lips as though I'm drowning.

Her touch is warm. Comforting. Harper continues rubbing my back, holding me, cradling me as the pain encompasses all of me.

Tears don't form.

I don't cry.

But my body wracks with pain. With grief. With fear and undeniable suffering. I've seen too much at the hands of my father. I don't want to become him, and yet I feel the changes surfacing.

I'm becoming the monster I never wanted to be.

The enemy is within me.

Harper is quiet and still, her arms around me like a fortress, giving me strength, hope and, more importantly, love.

At least it feels like it, but without the sentimental words.

She kisses the side of my head, holds me tight to her, and rubs at my back in a soothing motion that dulls the ache in my chest.

Eventually, I can breathe again.

Each breath is my own, and I feel foolish curled on the floor, my hands touching the ground that we walk on. I untangle from her embrace, silence between us.

I can't meet her stare.

Humiliation.

Embarrassment.

All of it burns through me, but the heat of anger has dissolved.

For now.

Harper shifts her weight but says nothing as I stand. Her hands are on my arms as she rises with me, her touch the only thread bringing me back to a harsh reality.

My gaze stares at her hand on my arm, but I can't bring her to move it, to push her away.

I don't embrace her either.

The silence hangs thick between us. Her touch is solid, warm, and strong. There's an ease that only she brings, which I find both comforting and curious.

She finally breaks the silence, her breath barely above a whisper. “Let’s go to bed.”

I nod, and she guides me to our bedroom in silence. She closes the door behind us while I head to the bed, my heart no longer raging as it had been moments earlier.

A quiet, serene relief floods through me as I climb into bed.

Harper does the same, remaining on her side, and she silently reaches for the pillows, the one rule I put into place when we shared the bed after our last fight.

Seems pointless now, considering what we did earlier this evening and tonight, her holding me tight.

I don’t want the pillows.

I don’t want the wall built up between us.

I want *her*.

I toss the extra pillows to the floor.

While I appreciate her giving me space, I no longer want it or need it.

I pull Harper against me, pushing my knee between her bare thighs, my leg finding her heated core.

She raises an eyebrow, and even in the darkness, I can see the hint of a smile on her lips. The pleasure that I can draw out of her with such a simple touch.

I'd do anything for this woman, *my wife.*

My lips crash on hers, my hands firmly plant against her cheeks, keeping her tight to me. I need her. Crave her.

My body seeks warmth and comfort, and Harper willingly obliges, parting her lips for me to gain entrance.

Her eyes fall shut, reveling in the feeling, and mine momentarily close while I kiss her, my lips dancing from her lips down her neck, worshipping every inch of her heated skin.

"Luca," she moans my name, her fingers tight in my hair as she drags my gaze up to hers. "I know you're hurting. I don't want to take advantage of you if this isn't what you want."

"Shut up and kiss me," I rasp, deepening the kiss, silencing her.

I need Harper.

She gives me something that I can't get elsewhere. She fulfills a need I never knew I had, buried deep within me.

Desperation gives way, and she offers me every bit of herself, once, twice, three times over. I worship her body like the temple that it is.

Every broken piece of me becomes whole when I'm with her, even as the darkness inside me threatens to take over. I feel that darkness edging closer, and she's the light that pushes it away.

The way she touches me grounds me, anchoring my heart to hers. There's nothing beyond the two of us —just heat, need, and desire. She is what I crave, what I need. There is no life worth living without her.

Everything else fades away—the pain, the doubts, the world outside our embrace. All I feel is Harper, her heartbeat in time with mine, her breath mingling with my own, creating a rhythm that is ours.

Every inch of her is beautiful and, more importantly, *mine.* I trace her skin with the pads of my fingers, memorizing every curve, every freckle, every magnificent detail that is uniquely Harper.

The sweet gasps and moans fill the air, which only encourages me further. Heat pools between her thighs with each stroke of my cock.

Her moans and pleas flood the room in ecstasy.

The connection between us is electric, sparking a fire that burns away any lingering uncertainty. She is my solace, my sanctuary, and I will never let her go.

I'm close, at the edge of the abyss, craving the feeling of falling with her, together.

She's nearly there with me. "Luca." Her moan is of desperation and neediness, which further quickens my pace, making my cock throb as I chase the orgasm with her.

My fingers rub at her clit, watching her face, studying every line and curve of her body as her hips buck off the mattress, back rising, toes curling, her entire body shudders as her hands clench at the sheets.

Her insides quiver and clench down onto my cock, the sensation overwhelming, bringing me over the edge with her. I struggle to keep my eyes open, but I want to see her come undone for me.

She's more beautiful than the aurora borealis on a winter night, more gorgeous than a sunrise on the peaks of the highest mountain.

I'd give up everything for her.

I'd burn the world down if it meant keeping her and Zeke safe.

Watching the glow of her cheeks, the smile on her lips, the gasp in her breath as she tries catching her orgasm on the chase toward oblivion, is the most beautiful vision.

She leans in, kissing me, her lips sweet and tasting like cherries as I wrap my arms around her, pulling her against me, and I grumble, realizing my mistake. "We didn't use a condom."

There's no fear in her voice, no concern, which gives me pause. "It's okay." Her hands smooth over my arms. "I'm on the pill."

Relief floods through me, and though I've heard her utter those words before, there's a sense of freedom in knowing that there won't be any more little ones running around, at least not until we're both ready.

FOURTEEN

ASHTON

The car ride back to the house could have been explosive. The tension was insurmountable, and Nova at least listened to me when I whispered that she needed to sit up front.

Thankfully, she didn't argue with me.

Luca storms into the house, slamming his bedroom door, making it clear he's still royally pissed at me.

Seems about right.

I don't know what it'll take for him to forgive me. Perhaps when he realizes that I do care about Nova.

She's more important to me than anyone I've ever been with, and there are a lot of girls on that roster.

I can understand why he's pissed.

He's worried about his little sister.

He thinks she's just another fuck, which is far from the truth.

I appreciate his concern. Believe it or not, had the tables been reversed, I'd have wanted to punch the living shit out of him too.

Thankfully, Brooks and Liam kept my face from getting bashed in and turning black and blue. I owe each of them.

Nova waltzes right into my bedroom. There's not even any attempt at sneaking in tonight. By the look on her face and the way she carries herself as she walks, she's still tipsy.

Damn.

I had a few drinks tonight, but Nova out-drank me. I didn't exactly count how many drinks she had, but the girl was drinking that punch like it was fruit juice and, well—the liquor did have a sweet taste to it.

Nova smiles, batting her long lashes up at me, those sky-blue eyes transfixing me in her gaze. "Are you mad at me?" she asks, her voice soft, fragile, almost child-like, which brings pause to the situation.

"Of course not." I collapse at the edge of my mattress, and Nova breathes a heady sigh of relief.

"Good." She strides closer, coming to straddle my hips as she settles her weight on my lap.

Her fingers tangle in my hair, her breath heavy with liquor, and I can't bring myself to go any farther tonight.

"You've had too much to drink." I drop a soft kiss to her cheek, my hands on her hips as I guide her off my lap.

Nova whimpers in protest. "I'm not drunk."

"You are very toasted." It's the nicest response I can give her because there's zero chance she's giving me consent tonight. And I need true, enthusiastic consent, not drunken, enthusiastic agreement.

After what transpired at the party, I'm not sure where we stand.

I like her.

She declared her love for me.

Well, she certainly shouted that she wants to marry me someday, which might as well be telling me that she loves me. Neither of us has used the L word yet.

If I wasn't slightly tipsy and she wasn't sloshed, we might be able to have a genuine conversation.

"I'm not drunk," Nova whines as she stands in front of me.

"Come on," I say, hoping I'm not making a huge ass mistake as I take her hand and head toward the bedroom door.

Quietly, I turn the doorknob; the squeak of the door causing me to wince.

I don't need Luca coming out of his bedroom, raging at me for sneaking across to Nova's room.

Although, technically it would be me putting Nova in her room, but I still don't think he'd be pleased when he witnesses her stumbling out of my room, drunk.

That's one fight I'd like to avoid.

I press a finger to my lips, reminding Nova to be quiet as we stalk across the hallway and I quietly open her bedroom door.

She's not particularly quiet with her footsteps or her breathing, which makes my heart hammer in my chest.

Luca is going to kill me.

I can hear him down the hallway, giving quite a tongue-lashing to Harper.

While I feel bad for her, right now I'm just glad it isn't me he's screaming at, because while I know he'd never hit a woman, he would most certainly take a swing at me.

We manage to sneak into Nova's bedroom, and I shut the door as quietly as possible, but the slight click makes me still for a moment.

No sign of Luca.

No doors slamming or footsteps pounding over the ground.

He's too busy fighting with Harper to notice me sneaking Nova back to her room.

I can breathe again.

Turning toward Nova, she's standing by her bed, head tilted, waiting diligently for me.

"Are you coming to bed?" she asks, and the smile on her face makes me eager to please her.

But I can't.

Not tonight.

Not while she's inebriated.

"I'm going to tuck you in," I say, hoping that will satisfy her.

Nova whimpers, and I swear the sound goes straight to my cock. My body responds like it always does to her, which makes everything a hell of a lot harder.

She's not going to make this easy on me, is she?

Nova draws back the sheets and unceremoniously strips down to nothing.

Fuck me.

I inhale sharply.

I want to stride across the room, cover her lips with mine, and take her.

But I can't, and I fucking hate my life right now.

If Luca hadn't been at the party, things might be different. She'd still be drunk, but at least I'd know she wants me. She's wanted me what feels like thousands of times before. But after what transpired, I can't be certain.

I need to hear it from her lips that we're okay.

That we'll get through this together.

That conversation has to come when she's sober.

When she has time to truly decide if I'm what she still wants after Luca's outburst.

Because I won't drive a wedge between her and her family.

"Are you coming ... to bed?" she says with a wicked smile. She knows exactly what she's doing to me, her perky breasts staring right at me, her pussy begging to be tasted.

My mouth is dry.

My cock throbbing to be touched by her hand, her lips, her pussy wrapped tight around my shaft.

"Climb into bed," I command.

The smile is ever-present on her face as she walks the two steps backward and lies down, waiting for me.

I know her bedroom like my own. I open the second drawer and grab a pair of pajamas for her to wear, bringing them to the bed.

"Clothes?" Her bright smile turns quickly into a scowl as she pouts.

"In case Zeke tears into your room in the morning." I help her get her arms into the tank top, and then she wiggles her pajama shorts on herself.

"I hate you," she grumbles at me.

I don't take her words to heart. I can't. Because if I did, they'd burn me, and I'd never get to sleep tonight.

"Lie back down." I shut off the bedroom light and then sit at the edge of her bed, the mattress dipping from my weight as I pull the covers up around her.

She huffs and rolls onto her side, facing away from me.

I can't tell if she's mad or acting angry because I made her put on her pajamas. I didn't intentionally reject her tonight, not in the way that she's certainly acting.

I'm just hoping it is her performing, and she's being her tenacious self and not truly mad at me.

"Scoot over," I whisper, and she shifts slightly, giving me barely enough room as I curl up behind her. The covers are an added layer between us, but I don't mind it tonight.

My arm drapes over her side, my breath against the back of her neck as I curl up against her body as best I can.

"You're such a tease," she mumbles. "Climb into bed with me. I promise I won't bite."

I laugh under my breath. "I might."

"You won't. You're all bark, especially tonight."

I playfully nibble at her neck, and she giggles, her hips grinding back against mine.

The heat builds, the room several degrees warmer. I have to stop. Her heart isn't a game, and I need another cold shower.

"Get some sleep," I whisper, kissing her cheek, my arms pulling her tighter against my chest.

"Hard to when I want to have sex with you," she purrs and rolls around to face me.

There's not a speck of tension between us, which at least helps me relax, but the fire still seems to burn within her tonight.

And I so desperately want to help her, but I can't.

I won't.

"You're tipsy," I remind her. She's more than slightly tipsy, but I'm trying to be nice and not make her feel like I'm outright rejecting her again. "You can't consent."

"Yes, I can," she grumbles and pushes me off her bed. The smile only grows on her face as I hit the floor, then the laughter starts in her chest, rumbling through her.

My eyes widen, praying that Luca won't come charging into her bedroom at any moment, because there's no way that he didn't hear my ass hit the floor.

Nova beams up at me. "I consent to you sleeping your lame ass on my floor while I fuck myself with my toy rabbit." She reaches for the nightstand and opens it.

God help me.

She turns the toy on, and the buzz fills the sound of the room.

She brings it between the sheets, moaning my name, and I can't take it anymore.

I leap off the floor, stumbling backward toward the door. I want to watch her touch herself, even give her a hand, but I can't. Not tonight.

"I'm going back to my room." I feel like a coward as I walk backward, my back gently hitting the door, and I sneak out and back into my room.

It's impossible to sleep, knowing what Nova is doing just across the hall.

And while I can't hear her toy rabbit buzzing and spinning, I know that damn toy is fucking her.

I want to be the one putting my cock between those sweet pussy lips and inching inside of her.

I collapse onto my bed, my body fueled with heat and steam. A cold shower would be good, but it also could wake Luca.

Well, fuck it.

It's late. Hopefully by now, he's in bed, asleep, and will leave me the fuck alone.

I head quietly for the bathroom, lock the door, turn on the fan, and blast the shower on cold. My cock throbs as I strip naked, and I can't stop myself from stroking it.

Knowing she's two doors down, pleasuring herself makes my pulse race. She's fucking herself, imagining that damn toy is me.

I'm her fantasy.

It's enough to make me rock hard, and I want to find release tonight.

Fuck the ice-cold shower.

I flip the faucet to hot, and steam begins to fill the shower stall.

I step under the hot spray, letting it cascade down my back while I stroke myself, eyes closing, imagining her lips, her tongue, her mouth taking every inch of me.

Fuck.

It isn't long before I'm reeling on the edge, and fuck, I'm ready to let myself go. There's no need to hang on, to drag the moment out any longer and torture myself.

My breath comes out in sharp bursts, the sound mixing with the water of the shower pounding over my back.

Heat overwhelms my senses as my cock pulsates in my hand, and with one hand, I reach for the shower wall, holding myself upright, while I imagine it's her mouth bringing me right over the edge, swallowing every drop that I have to offer.

My body tenses and trembles as heat coils low in my stomach. The thought of Nova touching herself only spurs me on, making the ache more intense. I bite down on my lower lip, forcing myself to stay quiet, not wanting anyone to hear my desperate need.

The blast of the shower turns cold as I finish, forcing me to shut off the spray as I'm panting hard, trying to catch my breath.

It's barely enough to satisfy the need Nova stirs inside of me, but it'll have to do for tonight.

In the early hours of the morning, I stir and sit up in bed when my bedroom door opens.

I glance at the clock. It's a few minutes after seven this morning, and the sun will be up soon. This time of year, it doesn't rise until nearly 7:45. I recognize that silhouette anywhere.

Nova.

"Can I climb into bed with you?" Her voice is tentative, and I pull back the covers, feeling a cold gust of air.

Nova climbs into my bed, and my arms instantly wrap around her as I shut my eyes, but I don't think I'll be able to fall back asleep.

I have less than twenty minutes until my alarm wakes me. I don't have hockey practice this morning, since we played last night, which afforded me a little extra sleep.

She curls her arms around me; they're chilly, and her body sends a shiver down my spine.

"You're freezing." I pull her closer, my legs tangling with hers in an attempt to warm her beneath the heat of the covers.

"It's these pajamas," she says with a smirk, laying her head on my pillow, sharing it as she rests her forehead against mine. "Are we okay?"

A faint smile tugs at my lips. My hands tug at her waist, holding her as tight as possible if that's any indication of my feelings for her. "I'm good." I inhale her intoxicating scent and close my eyes.

"Wake up, sleepyhead." She runs her fingers through my hair, playing with the strands.

Yawning, I smile, loving when she touches me, caresses me so casually that it feels natural and comforting. "I'm awake."

"Hardly." I can hear the smile in her voice.

I lazily open my eyes, staring at her wide, doe-like baby blues.

"Are we okay?" she asks me again.

"How are you feeling about Luca finding out about us?" I ask her, sensing her concern. The fact she's asked me twice now if we're okay makes me concerned that we might actually not be.

She emits a heavy sigh, staring off into the distance. "Stressed. He's my brother, I love him, but sometimes I want to strangle him. You know?"

Smiling and laughing softly, I nod. "Oh, I know." I lean closer, pressing my lips to her forehead, offering a reassuring kiss to her skin.

She curls farther into me, if that's at all possible, wrapping her arms around my waist. "I don't want him coming between us, but I also don't want to come between you two. You're best friends. Teammates." The worry lines etch on her face, and I feel the concern like a boulder in the pit of my stomach.

"I think we both need to find the time to talk to him."

"Separately, or together?" Nova asks.

"You know him better than I do." He might be my best friend, but they grew up together.

“Are you riding with him to Mom and Dad’s this weekend for Dante?” Nova asks.

“Unless he’s ditching me and making me take the bus, that was the plan.” I don’t know what Luca intends to do after class. We’re supposed to drive together, but for all I know, he could leave me on the side of the road. It wouldn’t be the first time.

“I’ll talk to him before he leaves for class, maybe I can grab breakfast with him. Then, you can talk to him in the car on the drive up?”

“It seems you’ve got it all figured out,” I whisper, dropping a soft kiss to her lips. I’m not sure talking to Luca on the drive to Dante’s is the best idea for me, but I keep that tidbit to myself. No sense in upsetting Nova or worrying her. I’ll find the time to talk to Luca this weekend, no doubt.

“I really don’t.” Nova’s bottom lip is pouty, and I lean in, kissing it. “You’ll be fine. We’ll be fine.” I want her to know that I’m not going anywhere.

“And if Luca doesn’t accept us together, what then?”

“That’s not an option. He’s your brother. He’s my best friend. He’ll just have to see how good we are together.” I try to sound convincing, but that thought flashed through my mind all night, making me restless and giving me strange dreams.

I pull her on top of me, loving the feel of her weight bearing down over me. I usually prefer dominating, but right now, just having her above me brings me comfort.

She straddles my waist and grabs my hands, pinning me against the mattress. "I hope I didn't scare you at the party."

Honestly, I wasn't sure exactly what she remembered, given how much she had to drink.

"You couldn't scare me." I stare up at her, feeling my breath catch in my throat.

Nova leans down and kisses me. I melt into her kiss, her body warm and sending tingles through me as she shifts her hips and grinds against me while deepening the kiss.

Fuck.

I break apart the kiss. As much as I want this, and boy, do I ever, I have to be up in less than five minutes for school, and she needs to talk to Luca. We don't need him barging in and witnessing the two of us doing dirty things to each other. It's bad enough Harper walked in and saw what she did.

"Tonight," I whisper, kissing her and rolling us over, pinning her beneath me. She murmurs as my lips mark her neck.

"You have to be with Luca tonight. At my parents' house."

I grumble, remembering our discussion just moments earlier, that I would be driving up with Luca. How easy it was to forget all of it when kissing her.

"Fuck, I hate it when you're right." I drop a quick kiss on her lips.

"I'm always right." Nova beams proudly, her hands at my lower back, embracing me. Her fingers begin trailing a soft pattern, dancing over my skin.

My alarm jars both of us, and she grumbles, climbing off me, knowing that it's time for both of us to be getting up. We have class together at nine, which gives Nova plenty of time to grab breakfast with Luca and try to talk to him before I'm stuck in the car with him.

FIFTEEN

NOVA

I quickly get dressed and grab my books for class, making sure I have everything so I don't have to stop back at the house.

Heading out of my room, I saunter into the kitchen. Zeke is eating breakfast, shoving bites of dry cereal into his mouth while Harper is glancing over one of her textbooks and eating a protein bar.

"Good morning," Harper says, a faint smile on her lips when she glances up at me. I can't decipher whether she and Luca are still fighting or not. She's not super chipper, but she doesn't look sullen, either.

"Morning. Is Luca still around? I was hoping to talk with him this morning."

"He's grabbing breakfast at the dining hall. He left about five minutes ago."

"I'll try to catch up with him." I sling my bag over my shoulder, hurry to slip on my shoes and coat, and head outside.

It's warmer this morning than yesterday, thankfully. The sidewalk is clear, and I take a shortcut through the neighbor's yard and hurry across campus. In under ten minutes, I'm at the dining hall, slightly out of breath from jogging. I'm not exactly out of shape; it's the ten pounds on my back—at least it feels like that—which makes it harder to run.

Catching my breath, I head into the dining hall, glancing around and spotting Luca grabbing a seat at a table alone. I hurry to grab some food for myself and then bring my tray over, hoping he'll let me join him. "This seat taken?"

Luca glances up from his breakfast, a piece of bacon in hand. He takes a bite and glances around. Is he looking for Ashton?

"It's just me." I don't wait for him to tell me I can sit with him. The question was more out of politeness than anything else. I place my tray down across from him on the table and slide out the chair, taking a seat.

"Good." He takes another bite, but I swear his jaw is grinding so friggin' tight that he's going to chip a tooth or two.

"I'm sorry we didn't tell you sooner." I hope my apology is enough to coax him. The irritation boils off of him like steam walloping at me.

He's hot and mad still.

"You should have told me, but I don't blame you." Luca grabs his glass of orange juice and takes a swig. "I blame Ashton."

Exhaling, I sigh and give a faint nod. "That's fair. He is your best friend." I'm trying to find a way to smooth things over, but I feel like I may have just set a match under Ashton instead.

"He *was* my best friend. Now, he's just a teammate." Luca forcefully puts the glass of juice down, splashing a bit onto the table. Thankfully, the glass doesn't shatter.

I don't dare ask if he's angry with Harper too. It was evident last night when he learned of her betrayal that he hurried home.

Another fight between them.

I don't know how long their marriage can last if they're constantly arguing. It seems like that's all they ever do, Luca mad at Harper over some secret that she's kept.

I suppose in this one, I'm a bit to blame.

I have to know. Wondering is killing me. "And Harper?"

His gaze shoots up at me. "What about her?" There's worry in his tone, and that causes me to raise an eyebrow.

"Are you still mad at her?"

"Harper and I are none of your business, Nova."

I can't help but laugh darkly at his words. "You're right. Harper and your relationship is none of my business, just like Ashton and me together has nothing to do with you."

His gaze tightens, realizing what he's said, and listening to me, it isn't quite what he was expecting. He leans back in his chair, staring at his food. I think I may have made him lose his appetite.

I'm still hungry. I eat my scrambled eggs and grab a piece of toast off my plate, munching on it, waiting for Luca to say something.

"My fight isn't with you, Nova."

It's not going exactly as I had planned. In fact, I'm worried I may have made things inadvertently worse for Ashton.

Shit.

"You don't have to fight with Ashton. There's no reason for it, Luca. We're both adults. He's been good to me. Ashton is sweet, kind; he's the perfect gentleman."

"Hardly," Luca grunts. "Have you seen how he treats the girls he sleeps with? One and done."

"That was before us." I hate defending his behavior. I'd seen how he treated women. I'm not oblivious to the fact that he's slept through probably a majority of the freshman and maybe even some of the sophomore class. “The girls were throwing themselves at him. I’ve seen them do the same thing to you.”

“But you don’t see me jumping into bed with them and then shoving them out the door after.”

“You can’t tell me you never did that.” I’m not an idiot. I know Luca has had his fair share of one-night stands. I don’t care what he did or what Ashton did, only what he does now.

“My past isn’t any of your concern.” Luca’s gaze narrows, and he shoves his tray slightly forward, clearly done. He didn’t eat as much as he usually would. It’s obvious that I’ve upset him, but I’m not sure how to fix this mess either.

“Look, I don’t want anything to come between you and Ashton. You’re best friends. That shouldn’t change.”

“He shouldn’t have fucked my little sister!”

A few heads turn, and I’m about ready to stab him with my fork if he doesn’t quiet his mouth. “We’re just practicing lines for our theater class!” I shout out to anyone who’s staring at us.

Luca raises an eyebrow but keeps his voice lower, quieter, giving us some privacy. It seems he doesn't want the entire school to know our business, either. Although anyone at the party is privy to it and, quite frankly, the entire hockey team already knows the drama. "I don't want to fight with you, Nova."

"So don't." I stare him in the eye, willing him to make peace with what's happening.

"Fine. You and I are good." His tone says otherwise.

"And Ashton?" I can't help but feel butterflies in my stomach.

He huffs and folds his arms across his chest. "He'd better watch his back this weekend."

SIXTEEN

LUCA

I still can't believe my little sister and my best friend are shacking up behind my back. It's not bad enough that I warned all of the hockey players on the team to stay away from her, but my best friend had to stab me in the back by screwing her and then keeping it a secret.

Of all the guys on the team, Ashton's past makes me the angriest about all of it.

Or maybe it's the fact that we're so tight and he chose not to tell me.

He had plenty of opportunities to come clean.

No, instead, he had to wait until he let Nova get drunk on her ass and make a huge announcement.

She embarrassed herself.

And while I'm not happy that Harper kept the truth from me, I can see where she would feel it wasn't her secret to tell.

I've forgiven her.

I've mildly forgiven Nova. She's young, foolish, and never been in love. She's barely an adult; she just turned eighteen. She has an excuse.

There is zero excuse for Ashton.

He didn't heed my warning.

No, instead, he blatantly chose to fuck my little sister and then lie about it. If he were a man, he'd have come clean immediately after it happened, told me the truth, confessed that he'd slept with her.

Maybe I could have forgiven him.

It's the lying.

The betrayal.

The fact we live under the same roof and for months he kept it a secret, like she wasn't good enough to tell anyone they were dating.

That sickens me.

Nova deserves better.

My little sister deserves a man who will shout from the rooftops that he likes her, wants to be with her.

Clearly, that's not Ashton.

After classes, I head back to the house to help with dinner. Harper's already in the kitchen, and Zeke is banging the extra pots and pans, pretending to help as he sits on the floor.

"How about I take over the cooking?" I offer, letting her look after Zeke.

"Are you sure? I'm almost done with the prep. It just has to go in the oven." She's cutting the potatoes, and the baby carrots are already sliced in half. There's chicken in some type of glaze, and she's popping the potatoes and carrots on a separate tray. She glances at the cookbook, following the recipe, which remarkably looks like it might be similar.

"We could have just eaten on campus tonight." I drop a quick kiss on her cheek. I've never seen her cook before, but I honestly like this side of her.

"I know, but lately, we've been having dinner with your family on Friday nights. I thought it might be nice for me to try to cook us a real dinner instead of having the same stuff at the dining hall. I just hope it turns out."

"I'm not worried. It looks good."

"It'll look better when it's done in the oven." She puts the vegetables in first and sets the timer on the stove.

"What can I do to help?" I ask.

"Would you mind watching Zeke for a bit? I'm going to have him all weekend. It'd be nice to have a few minutes' break."

The words come out before I even think about what I'm saying. "You could come with us and stay at my parents' this weekend. They have a room for Zeke. Mom could help you with him? She loves him so much."

Harper inhales sharply and forces a smile. I see the hesitation, and I should know better than to suggest visiting my parents.

They're mafia.

Dangerous.

Deadly.

Even suggesting that she come to stay is a terrible idea.

"Sorry," I wince. "I wasn't thinking."

Harper's forced smile weakens, and she steps forward. Standing on her tiptoes, she presses a kiss to my lips. "I appreciate the offer, but I'm going to have to pass. I'll stay here this weekend."

"It'll be quiet; it'll just be Nova, Liam, and you two." I nod toward Zeke.

She smiles and shakes her head. "Nothing is quiet with this guy." Bending down, Harper scoops Zeke up into her arms, giving him kisses.

He pushes her away and then throws out his arms for me.

I hesitate, not because I don't adore the kid, but because I'm afraid to get too attached. He's Harper's son. I don't want to destroy him.

There are flashes I get, memories of my father, and I see myself in him more and more. I don't want to be like Dante, and I certainly don't want to hurt Zeke. But being forced to work for the man I despised all my life, how can I not become him?

"Luca?" Harper's voice jars me as she sees Zeke trying to reach for me and my hesitation.

This time, I'm the one forcing the smile as I take him in my arms. "Take a break. I've got him."

Her brow furrows as she rubs Zeke's back. "Are you sure? If he's too much, I can take him back."

I chuckle. "I don't think the kid comes with a return receipt."

Her nose crinkles, and Harper smiles. This time, it's genuine.

I love her laugh. I adore that smile with her dimple on her left cheek. Her dark eyes glisten, and I swear there are gold flecks that shimmer from the sunlight cast in through the window.

"We are definitely past the return window," Harper jokes and then crinkles her nose at the scent wafting from the little man in my arms. "Oh no. Diaper duty. Here, let me take him."

Zeke giggles like he's proud of the smell emanating from him. It's grotesque, but when does *that* ever smell pleasant?

"It's fine. I know how to change a diaper. I'll handle it." I carry Zeke to his room, and Harper follows.

"Are you sure?" she asks, watching me from the doorjamb.

Does she not trust me with Zeke?

I wouldn't blame her.

I place Zeke on the changing table and quickly change his diaper.

The stove beeps, and Harper leaves the two of us alone while I finish the diaper change before bringing him to the bathroom so I can wash my hands.

"Did you leave the diaper in his bedroom?" Harper asks me from the bathroom. I left the door open, and she's already on me like I'm incapable of handling a simple diaper change.

I'd be annoyed if it were anyone else.

"It's in the diaper pail. I know how to look after Zeke." I kiss his forehead, and he wiggles away from me, wanting to get down. I gently set his feet on the ground, and he tears off, arms out, running around like a little monster.

"Dragon! Roar!" Zeke shrieks with laughter, running around the living room. While his words aren't crystal clear, I've learned to decipher most of his babbling over the past couple of weeks.

Nova pokes her head out of her bedroom. "Is the little dragon okay?"

"He's fine!" Harper shouts over the roar of the little dragon running wild. "Sorry for the noise."

Nova's been studying for hours or, more likely, avoiding me. It's fine; I'm leaving for Dante's soon. She'll have the house all weekend, and thankfully, Ashton will be with me, so I won't have to worry about the two of them getting up to trouble.

Ashton hasn't come home yet. I expect he'll be back in time for us to leave. We've exchanged a few brief texts, him double-checking that he has a ride tonight.

I'm feeling generous.

I won't make him walk or take the bus.

"I made enough dinner, you're welcome to join us when it's ready," Harper says, inviting Nova to dine with us.

When the timer beeps again and this time dinner is ready, Nova finds her way out of her books and to the table for dinner.

"Thanks. This smells amazing. Way better than the chicken tenders at school."

We all sit down, minus Ashton, for dinner. He's probably at the dining hall. Liam joins us, although he's a bit quieter than usual. I'm assuming he also knew about Nova and Ashton and is trying to keep the peace or at least stay on my good side.

Dinner is delicious. I don't want to move from my seat at the table, but I hear the front door and glance at my watch. It's time to head to Dante's. Although we won't begin any training this evening, we'll likely be getting started early tomorrow morning.

I'd rather sleep in my bed with Harper and wake up extra early and drive over, but that isn't an option. Dante has made it clear that he expects me to stay weekends, unless there's a hockey game.

I hate playing Thursday games.

It means longer weekends and more time learning about the ins and outs of the mafia.

I've mastered the gun range, which wasn't the worst thing in the world. But knowing that I need to know how to use a gun, how to shoot someone—that, I find far more unsettling.

I give Harper a kiss goodbye and kiss Zeke on the cheek before grabbing my weekend bag and departing.

It's cold outside, the crisp air allowing me to see my breath as we walk to the car.

Ashton says nothing.

No apology.

No words.

He's silent, which irks me even further.

I throw my bag into the backseat. Ashton does the same, and then we climb into the car.

We drive, the radio on, the only noise between us.

He doesn't even try to explain himself. Although I'm not sure I'd listen, either.

I've made up my mind; I'm pissed at him.

He deserves my wrath for what he's done.

We ride in silence all the way up to the compound. I punch in the code at the front gate, and the wrought-iron fence opens.

It's slow, takes several long drawn-out seconds before I hit the gas and pull up out front.

Heading out of the car, Dante greets us, which I find quite unusual.

"Luca," he says, and there's a smile on his face, but I'm not buying it.

He's never happy to see me. I'm the son he wishes he never had. I'm sure if Mom got pregnant with another child, he'd be gleeful that he might be able to manipulate and control him, make him the heir to the Ricci empire.

That's not me, and yet, here I am, forced to work under Dante.

"Come on inside; we have quite a bit to discuss." Dante gestures for us to follow as he heads up the front stairs and opens the door, granting us entrance inside the compound.

I leave my bag just inside the door, take off my shoes and winter coat. The house is plenty warm, a little too warm for my liking. Practically like I'm in hell. Maybe I am. Dante is the devil.

"I thought we were starting work in the morning." Ashton is right on my heel and he steps beside me, placing his bag on the opposite side of the door before hanging up his coat and removing his shoes.

"I have a reconnaissance mission, and unfortunately, these types of jobs happen under the cover of night." Dante leads us farther into the house, to his office.

Ashton and I step inside. I barely glance at him, the tension thick between us.

"Tell us about the assignment." Ashton is the first to speak, not the least bit reluctant to get started on a mission.

At this point, I haven't been forced to do much. Learning to shoot wasn't exactly a fun assignment, but I wasn't killing anyone. I was hitting a target. Now, I'm pretty good at it, but I hope that's not going to be part of our next task.

"As you know, we control a certain territory. Someone has been smuggling goods just outside of Blue Sky Resort." Dante pulls up a map on his phone, showing us the location. "This dirt road is hardly ever used, especially in winter. Well, it turns out that's where their operation is. At the end of the road, there's an old building that's been shuttered. I need you both to do some surveillance work, take some photographs, find out exactly what they're smuggling. Is it drugs or weapons? I need to know as much as I can, how many men there are, bring me back details. Can you both handle that?"

"Yes, sir." Ashton is quick to agree to help.

"Yeah, we can handle surveillance. Is there a location where we should be hiding?" Since we aren't familiar with the terrain, I don't want us to be spotted.

"I don't have enough information to help with that, just stay out of sight. Kill the lights on the car, park and hide the vehicle, if you have to, and travel on foot the rest of the way. I'm sure you both can use your heads and figure out the best way to get intel. The shipment happens around midnight. You're dismissed."

Dante hands Ashton a folder with information. There isn't much, but it does detail the information that Dante is looking for, and there's a place to mark in as much information as possible.

We head out of his office and retrieve our shoes and coats, heading back into the car.

While it's not anywhere near midnight yet, we certainly don't want to show up, lights blazing, car rumbling, and alert everyone of our presence.

"Did Dante give us anything in that file?" My attention is on the road, which at least it's not snowing tonight. It's cold, freezing enough to see one's breath outside.

Ashton flips through the pages.

"Not much. Mostly, it's what he wants us to fill in."

I press the button on my car door and roll down my window.

"It's fucking cold!" Ashton scowls at me. He reaches for the heater, cranking the temperature in the car.

Smirking, I grab the folder from his hand and toss it out the window.

"Are you fucking insane? We need that."

I press the button on the door, rolling the window back up. "We're not here to take fucking notes for him. We'll surveil and get out. This isn't a school assignment."

Ashton grumbles under his breath.

"What's that?" I glance in his direction.

He folds his arms across his chest. "You've been a dick since you found out I'm dating Nova."

A dark laugh bubbles and seeps out past my lips. "You think *that's* why I'm angry with you?"

Ashton shifts in the front seat. "Isn't it?"

"You broke the one cardinal rule that I had regarding Nova and then you proceeded to lie to me for months!" I keep my gaze trained on the road, but I want to pull over, throw Ashton out, let him fend for himself.

"Nova is old enough to make her own decisions. She's not a child anymore, and you need to stop treating her like one."

"I'm not treating her like a child. She just turned eighteen. Did you even wait until she was legal or were you—"

He interrupts me. "I didn't touch your sister until she consented."

"You didn't answer my question." My jaw clenches.

"She was eighteen. I swear I never laid a finger on her until she was of age."

"Still doesn't make it any better," I grumble and glare at him. "You were warned to stay away from her!"

"I can't help my feelings for Nova. Yes, you told everyone on the team she wasn't some girl to fuck around with. My feelings for her are genuine. We hang out all the time; you've seen that, the flirting, the other stuff, it just developed on its own." Ashton's voice is calm, but I don't feel the least bit calm, listening to him tell me about Nova.

"You only think those feelings are genuine because you've never experienced them before. What happens when you meet another girl who knocks your socks off? You'll break Nova's heart, and I'll be left picking up the pieces." I don't want to see my little sister getting hurt by my best friend.

"Okay, I know I may have made a few mistakes in the past with girls—"

"A few?" I laugh at his exaggeration of a few. He's slept with tons of girls, more than I can keep track, and I doubt that Ashton even knows how many girls in total he's bedded.

"I've fucked up, but that doesn't mean I'm going to keep screwing up."

"Seems like it to me. That's all you've ever done, Ashton. You're Captain of the Fuck a Girl Squad."

He doesn't so much as flinch. "That's not even a thing. And no one calls me that."

"The *team* calls you that."

"Liar." Ashton glances at me. "Admit it. You're just jealous of what Nova and I have."

Has he lost his mind? "You're kidding me. I can attest I'm not the least bit jealous of your relationship *with my sister.*"

I glance at him, and he shrugs. "Semantics. You know what I mean. What we share, the fact we're close and can tell each other everything. There are no secrets between us. We both actually like each other and can stand to be in the same room together."

I flinch at his mention of *secrets*. That's what's been tearing Harper and me apart at every turn. When things finally get back on track, there are new secrets, new surprises that seem to want to find their way to destroy our relationship.

Not this time.

Not anymore.

I won't let anything or anyone come between Harper and me.

Exhaling a heavy sigh, I make the turn-off for the road for our mission. It's nearly two hours to midnight, which should give us plenty of time to scope out the area without being seen.

The clouds are thick, the sky black as night.

The road is covered in snow, but the path already has several tire tracks heading up the desolate road.

"Kill the lights," Ashton commands, as if I take orders from *him*.

"And run us off the road? No, thanks. And our conversation isn't done." It's too dark to shut off the headlights and safely make it up the narrow road.

"Wouldn't dream of it ending now," Ashton seethes. "Don't worry, if you want to go at it on the ice, I'm game."

"Are you really going to fight me? You know I'll kick your ass, Rinaldi."

He's got some nerve! After betraying me and hooking up with my little sister, now he wants to fight me?

He laughs, shaking his head. "Do you really think you can take me?"

"Wouldn't be the first time." I shoot daggers at him as I attempt to keep my focus on the one-lane road.

"That's rich, you thinking that you've ever beaten me. I let you win, Ricci." The smug sound of his voice sickens me.

He's so full of shit. "Is that what you're telling yourself?"

I climb the mountain slowly, not wanting the roar of the engine to alert anyone of our presence. But I swear the shouting match between us is far louder than any hum of the vehicle.

At least it's dead outside and the middle of the night.

We crest to the top where it's flat. On our approach is the battered building of what used to be a cabin. It's abandoned, dark, and run-down.

"You ever touch my sister again, I'll end you with my bare hands."

"She's not yours to protect. Not anymore," Ashton grinds. "She's mine. I'm hers. You're just her older, annoying brother who is interfering in her life."

"Get the fuck out of my car." I hit the brakes

forcefully, the wheels spinning on ice, kicking up sludge.

Ashton shoots off another order, ignoring my command. "Turn around. We're out in the open. We can't park here."

I ignore him. "Get. The. Fuck. Out." Heat burns my cheeks, and I grip the steering wheel so tight, I wonder if I might peel off the leather.

"Gladly. By the way, Nova will hate you when I call her and tell her what a dick you are." Ashton yanks open the door and steps out.

"Tattletale."

The cold air whirls into the car. It's frigid, the night air a reminder of the job we're here to do.

My stomach plummets.

"Ashton—"

"Fuck off, Ricci." Ashton slams the car door shut, slinking off into the darkness.

I can't chase after him and leave the car abandoned in front of the cabin.

I make a three-point turn on the narrow road and turn around. Glancing at the clock, we have less than an hour until the real fun begins. It took longer to climb up the mountain than I anticipated.

And I just left Ashton out in the open, in the cold, alone.

It doesn't take minutes for shame to build within me, merely seconds.

Regret.

But I can't park out in the open, not without being seen.

Ashton can manage on his own for twenty minutes while I figure out where the hell to park the car and hike back up the road, unseen.

The headlights of my car reveal a ravine on either side as I slowly descend down the path which we came.

Desperately, I need to find a side road, somewhere to park, and I can head the rest of the way on foot, catch up with Ashton.

But there wasn't anything I noticed on the way up.

We were also arguing, which didn't exactly mean my head was screwed on tight.

I'll have to pay closer attention coming back down the slushy road.

Slowly making my way down the one-lane road, headlights reflect off the trees in the distance.

Shit.

It's another vehicle coming up the road.

I tap the brakes and slide across the icy road and turn the wheel, keeping from falling into the ravine.

My stomach is in my chest, and I curse under my breath.

The vehicle in front of me revs their engine and pushes forward, having spotted me. They turn their brights on, blinding me.

I have little choice but to put my car in reverse. I floor the gas, driving backward, watching over my shoulder as I dangerously navigate the edge of the mountainside and the narrow one-lane road in the snow, until I'm back in front of the battered cabin.

Not fucking ideal.

So much for being inconspicuous.

Where the hell is Ashton?

I grab for my phone and attempt to call Dante, but the call immediately fails.

Men flood out of the vehicle in front of me, blocking the road, guns drawn. The car's engine is idle with its headlights blinding me.

A darkened figure steps out, the man who was sitting behind the driver, smoking a cigarette. It dangles from his lips as he lifts his right hand, giving a gesture to move in.

Two men I don't recognize come to my driver-side door, smash open my car window, throw open my door, and yank me out of the vehicle.

I'm entirely at their mercy.

To Be Continued...

The story continues in Between Sin and Silence (Crimson Ice Book 4).

In the darkened underworld of the mafia, silence cannot save you.

And threats become the new reality.

Luca and Ashton are in danger.

Danger from the mission Dante sent them on.

And threats from the enemy, who desire to destroy Luca's new family.

Mafia protection is born in silence...

Love thy enemy...

Liam Moretti can't get the kiss with Bristol Greyson out of his head. It never should have happened.

She's the enemy, a girl he grew up knowing and despising.

But one unexpected kiss lands him craving more...

Hate thy self...

Bristol has mysteries of her own, surrounding not only her heart but her body.

Broken.

Troubled.

Sick.

One kiss won't cure her, but could it kill her?

Silence is filled with sin when secrets are kept from those you care most about...

SHOP SIGNED AND EXCLUSIVE EDITIONS

THANK you so much for reading Between Fire and Frost. I hope you enjoyed the novel. Be sure to sign up for my newsletter for up-to-date new release details, sales, early release news, and more!

If you love signed paperbacks, special edition books, or discounted book bundles be sure to check out my online bookshop: https://shopwillowfox.com

ABOUT THE AUTHOR

Willow Fox has written in multiple genres. She's written everything from young adult dystopian to spicy RomCom novels. Her books have been translated into five languages and sold across the world.

Whether Willow is writing romance or sitting outside by the bonfire reading a good book, she loves the magic of the written word.

Follow her on any of her social media sites or through her newsletter!

Willow also writes kinky romance books under the pen name Allison West.

Visit her website at:

shopwillowfox.com

ALSO BY WILLOW FOX

Eagle Tactical Series

Expose: Jaxson

Stealth: Mason

Conceal: Lincoln

Covert: Jayden

Truce: Declan

Mafia Marriages

Secret Vow

Captive Vow

Savage Vow

Unwilling Vow

Ruthless Vow

Bratva Brothers

Brutal Boss

Wicked Boss

Possessive Boss

Obsessive Boss

Dangerous Boss

Bossy Single Dad Series

Billionaire Grump

Mountain Grump

Bachelor Grump

Ice Dragons Hockey Romance

Faking it with the Billionaire

Daring the Hockey Player

Arresting the Hockey Player

Crimson Ice

Between Blades and Blood

Between Ice and Oaths

Between Fire and Frost

Between Sin and Silence

Between Steel and Secrets

Want more kinky romance? I also write under the pen name Allison West.

Gem Apocalypse Series

Emerald Rebellion

Amber Voyeur

Sapphire Sacrifice

Scarlet Assassin

Crimson Crown

Royally Claimed Series

Palace Secrets

Maiden Claimed

Grave Misfortune

Academy of Littles

Little Etta

Little Gigi

Little Eliza

Reforming the Rebellious

Little Lizzie's Reform (Little Lizzie)

Little Prim and Proper (Little Kat)

Virtue and Vice

A Proper Punishment (Little Lena)

Little Brides (Little Clara)

Dowries and Deception

Delia's Debt (Little Delia)

Decoy Bride (Little Vera)

Jessie's Secret

Violet's Penance

Piper's Escape

Fiery Luna

Little Jade

Little Alice

Little Love Bundle/Western Daddies

Little Samantha

Little Lexa

Little Autumn

Little Rosie

Prefer a sweeter romance with action and adventure? Check out these titles under the name Ruth Silver.

Aberrant Series

Love Forbidden

Secrets Forbidden

Magic Forbidden

Escape Forbidden

Refuge Forbidden

Nightblood

Royal Reaper

Stolen Art

www.ingramcontent.com/pod-product-compliance
Lightning Source LLC
La Vergne TN
LVHW100513110826
845146LV00002B/626

9798886372823